The Rusty Old Car

Margaret Gregory

Also by Margaret Gregory

TYMOREAN TRUST SERIES
THE THIRD GENERATION SERIES
ATAPI SORCERESS SERIES
MAEVEN DRAGON THIEF SERIES
TOUCHING OTHER LIVES SERIES

Table of Contents

Chapter 1: The Discovery of the Past

The sun hung low over the hills of Mill Haven, casting a golden hue across the landscape as the laughter of three friends echoed through the late afternoon air. Noah reclined on the grass, his head propped on his arms behind him, gazing up at the cotton candy clouds drifting lazily overhead. A gentle breeze rustled the wildflowers that dotted the hillside, their vibrant colours a stark contrast to the dull, worn fabric of his old band t-shirt. He felt a sense of ease—one that was all too rare in the confines of his everyday life.

"Are you two even paying attention?" Tessa teased, a playful glint in her bright green eyes. She sat cross-legged next to Noah, her athletic build accentuated by her practical shorts and a fitted tank top that showed off her toned arms. "I could be talking about the next big game, and you'd be too busy staring at the clouds."

"Maybe I'm just considering the vastness of the universe," Noah shot back, grinning. "Or wondering if you'll ever stop talking about sports."

"Hey, I have a right to be excited!" Tessa laughed, her curls bouncing as she leaned back, arms stretched wide as if to embrace the sky. "Plus, my athletics team is going to the championships this year, and you know what that means."

Mia, sitting a few feet away, looked up from her sketchbook, her dark hair tied back in a messy ponytail. The corner of her mouth quirked into a smile, though her almond-shaped eyes held a glimmer of something more serious. "It means I'll be hearing about it for the next six months. The season has only just started," she quipped, her voice light yet laced with genuine affection. She flipped the page of her sketchbook, revealing a half-finished drawing of the view before them—a swirling mix of blues, greens, and the soft yellows of the wildflowers.

"I'll take that as a compliment," Tessa replied, nudging Noah with her elbow. "You should be grateful I'm not dragging you two along to practice."

"Grateful? Sure," Noah said, his tone teasing. He didn't point out he was usually working when she had practice.

Mia chuckled, her laughter like a soft melody floating in the warm air. "You know," she said, tilting her head thoughtfully, "there are more important things than sports."

"Not for me," Tessa proclaimed.

"Like what?" Noah inquired, tilting his head in curiosity.

"Like... hidden treasures," she said, her eyes suddenly brightening with excitement. "Don't you remember all those stories about the old ghost towns and forgotten places around here? I swear there's an entire history buried in Mill Haven. Don't you care about the lives people lived before you were born?"

"Boring history," Tessa said, rolling her eyes. But her tone was playful, and she nudged Mia again with a conspiratorial grin. "You're not suggesting we actually go looking for ghosts, are you?"

Noah sat up, suddenly animated. "Why not? What's the worst that could happen? We might find something cool! I mean, they did have a minor gold rush out this way. I don't know about ghost towns, but there are old shacks in the hills with only the stone chimneys left and some of the houses west of town were built on old abandoned shacks."

"Or we might find a ghost," Tessa countered, pretending to shiver dramatically. "No one lives in those old houses now. If anything is left there it's likely just junk."

"Come on, Tessa," Mia chimed in, her enthusiasm infectious. "We could explore the outskirts of town. I heard there's a shunned field not far from here."

"A shunned field?" Tessa raised an eyebrow, scepticism etching her features. "Who have you been listening to? It's probably Parson's Folly. It was where the old miners dumped their rubbish. It sounds like a perfect place to get lost or, worse, step in something gross."

"Or discover a hidden treasure," Noah suggested, his hazel eyes sparkling with mischief. "Imagine what we could find! Old artefacts for instance. There's that old burnt out car there, the one Old Clarrie at the garage reckons is Clara's car."

Mia's expression shifted, a flicker of something unnameable

crossing her face, but she quickly masked it with a grin. "You mean it's just sitting there, rusting away? That could be cool. Maybe I will draw it."

"See?" Noah urged, nudging Tessa, bolstered by Mia's interest. "We could make a day of it. We could even take some snacks."

"Okay, why not? Haven't you ever been out there, Mia?" Tessa relented, though her tone remained cautious. "But I warn you now, if we find a ghost, I'm blaming you."

"Deal!" Noah shot back, springing to his feet, his excitement palpable. "Let's do it. We've still got an hour before it gets dark."

As they made their way down the hillside, the laughter and banter started to fade, replaced by a sense of anticipation. The tall grass brushed against their legs, and the sweet scent of wildflowers filled the air, mingling with the earthy aroma of sun-warmed soil. The path they followed wound through a thicket of trees, their leaves whispering secrets to one another as the trio ventured deeper into the unknown.

"Hey, remember when we used to play in these woods?" Noah asked, nostalgia creeping into his voice.

"Of course," Tessa said, a hint of longing in her tone. "We thought we were explorers, searching for hidden caves and treasures."

"Yeah, and the only treasure we found was that old tyre in the creek," Mia added, her voice light. She hadn't been in Mill Haven very long back then.

"And we thought it was a gold mine," Noah laughed, shaking his head at the memory.

Soon they reached the edge of the field—an expanse of tall grass and low bushes that swayed in the breeze like waves rolling over the ocean. The vibrant greens and yellows danced under the sun, creating a picturesque scene, but something about it felt eerily untouched, as if time itself had forgotten this place.

"Wow," Tessa breathed, taking in the view before them. "This is... kind of beautiful. I remember this place as barren. The town really did a good job here."

"Right?" Noah said, stepping forward and squinting into the distance. "I think I see something over there. Come on!"

They made their way through the grass, laughter bubbling up again as they raced each other, their competitive spirits ignited. But as they drew nearer, the laughter subsided, replaced by an air of curiosity and awe.

There, half-hidden among scattered wildflowers and some low scrubby bushes, stood the rusty old car. Its once-vibrant paint had been blackened by fire, and was now covered in patches of rust, giving it an air of melancholy. It was a relic of the past—a time capsule frozen in a moment of decay.

"Whoa," Noah whispered, stepping closer, his fingers brushing against the cold metal. "This is it. It's an old Holden Gemini. I wonder why they left it here when they filled this area in."

"Probably as a home for the local wildlife," Tessa suggested, when a fox sped out from a hole along the side. The car itself was partly sunken in the dirt.

Mia approached with a sense of reverence, her gaze fixed on the vehicle. "It's... beautiful in a way," she murmured, her voice barely above a whisper.

"More like creepy," Tessa replied, crossing her arms. "What even happened here? I mean, the car is in the middle of the field, nowhere near a road. If it was Clara's, why is it here? Whatever happened to her?"

Noah shrugged, glancing from Mia's odd absorption and back at Tessa. "Maybe it has a story to tell. We could check it out."

Mia stepped forward, her heart racing. She reached out a hand, hesitant but drawn to the worn steering wheel like a moth to a flame. As her fingers made contact, a wave of energy coursed through her, and the world around her faded away.

A kaleidoscope of images flooded her mind— voices raised in anger, flashes of a tragic accident, a face covered in blood, leaning over the steering wheel, and a fleeting glimpse of the ghost white face of a girl who could have been Clara, the car's owner. Mia gasped, her vision swirling with emotions that weren't her own. A pulse of panic struck her heart; she staggered back, breathless and wide-eyed.

"Mia?" Noah's voice pierced through the haze, filled with concern. "Mia, what's wrong?"

"I saw... there was an accident," she stammered, gripping the side of the car for support. "Someone was hurt..."

"Mia," Tessa urged, her voice tight with worry. "What else did you see? Are you okay?"

Noah stepped closer, placing a comforting arm around Mia's shoulder. "You don't have to talk about it if you don't want to."

But Mia's mind raced, echoes of the past reverberating in her thoughts. "I saw her," she whispered, trembling. "I saw Clara."

Tension hung in the air, thick and heavy, as the reality of what they had stumbled upon began to settle in. The playful day had shifted, morphing into something darker—a mystery that demanded to be uncovered.

"Mia, are you sure it was her?" Tessa pressed, her protective instincts flaring. "She disappeared years ago, when we were just little kids. No one knows what happened to her."

Mia's heart pounded in her chest, but beneath that fear was a flicker of determination. "We have to find out what happened here," she whispered, her voice steadying as she glanced between her friends. "We have to."

Noah and Tessa exchanged looks, an unspoken agreement passing between them. They stood together, a trio bound by friendship and now by a shared mission.

"Alright," Noah said, his voice filled with resolve. "Let's uncover the truth. I know there is a plaque under that picture of hers at school that made me think she was dead. No dates or details. Though it had to be after she left school. What if we check the back issues of the local paper? They have them online now. We can do a search on her name."

"I'll try the bigger paper," Tessa decided.

Mia let them search, she was drawn to look up at the old road that circled the field. A tree caught her eye, standing like a stoic sentinel. An ancient oak tree. She took out the sketch book she always carried and began to draw – the edge of the wrecked car, the long way up to the road, and without realising it, adding a shadowy figure standing beside the tree, a silhouette against the lowering sun.

A faint gust of a cooler breeze caused them to remember the time. It seemed the air buzzed with an electric tension.

Noah murmured, "Clara's parents died not long before she disappeared. The police believed she was in her car when it left the road – right where her parents had gone off the road. Kaelen Evans was found dead, but no sign of her."

Tessa added, "I didn't know her father was a policeman. They really played up her disappearance, and had a picture in the paper asking if people saw her. Like she might have lost her memory and wandered off. Then after a week, the story died out."

As they formed a semi-circle around the car, the sun dipped lower in the sky, casting long shadows that danced among the wildflowers and waving grass. Each of them now feeling the weight of their discovery. And at that moment, in the fading light of day, they knew they were on the brink of something important - an exploration not just of the past but of themselves, as they decided to unravel the threads of a mystery that had long been forgotten.

Chapter 2: Whispers of Clara

The bell above the door of the Mill Haven Diner chimed cheerfully as Noah, Mia, and Tessa stepped inside, the warmth of the sun outside giving way to the comforting buzz of conversation and the rich scent of freshly brewed coffee. The diner was full, as it often was on a Saturday morning, with families gathered around booths and couples sharing intimate breakfasts. The walls were adorned with faded photographs of the town's history, each frame a portal to a time long past, and the chatter of patrons mixed with the occasional clatter of dishes being cleared.

"Right here, guys!" Tessa called out, waving her arm to catch their attention. She had already secured a booth in the far corner, its red vinyl seats still holding the remnants of countless conversations and laughter. Noah and Mia made their way through the maze of tables, their excitement palpable.

"I can't believe that was actually Clara's car," Mia said, her voice barely above a whisper, as if speaking too loudly might shatter the fragile mystery surrounding the vehicle. She slid into the booth, her dark ponytail swinging as she settled in, her almond-shaped eyes wide with anticipation. "Why was it just sitting there? Surely the police would have hauled it away to check it over."

Noah said, "They said Kaelen had been drinking, and had been arguing before he took off." He shrugged, his hazel eyes darting around the diner, catching snippets of conversations and laughter. "I don't know. But if Clara had also been in the car, we should find out everything we can. She is still missing and there's got to be a reason the car has been abandoned like that."

Tessa leaned forward, resting her forearms on the table, her bright green eyes sparkling with a mix of determination and mischief. "We should go to the library later and ask Mrs. Jenkins. She knows everything about Mill Haven's history. If anyone can help us, it's her."

Mia nodded, but her gaze drifted to the window, where sunlight danced on the pavement outside. "What if the town doesn't want us digging up the past? Clara's disappearance... it's like a wound they don't want to reopen."

"Then we'll just have to be careful," Noah replied, his voice steady but his brow furrowed in thought. "We have to respect what happened, but we can't let fear stop us from finding the truth."

The waitress approached, her notepad poised and ready. "Morning, kids! What can I get you?" She wore a friendly smile, her hair pulled back in a messy bun, and a smudge of flour dusted her apron.

"Three coffees, please," Tessa said, her tone brightening as she glanced at the menu. "And I'll have the blueberry pancakes."

Mia hesitated, her fingers tracing the edge of the table. "I think I'll just have a bagel... maybe with cream cheese?"

"And I'll have the breakfast burrito," Noah added, forcing a smile. "Thanks."

As the waitress moved away, Tessa leaned in closer, her voice low. "I overheard some of the older folk talking in the park the other day. I was taking a breather near the kiosk. The one with the mural. A couple of others were looking at it, and one told the other that it was painted by the town mystery. Clara's name was mentioned. The old folk went quiet when her name came up, like they were scared or something. We need to know what made them act like that."

Mia's heart raced at the thought. "What if Clara's story is something someone wants to hide? What if it's dangerous?"

Noah reached across the table, placing his hand on hers. "We can handle it. We're in this together."

The waitress returned with steaming mugs and plates, setting them down with a clatter. "Here you go! Enjoy!"

As they dug into their food, the conversation flowed, but the initial excitement was tinged with an undercurrent of anxiety. The food was comforting, the pancakes fluffy and syrupy, but the weight of Clara's absence hung between them like an uninvited guest.

After finishing their meal, the trio cut through the park on the way to the Mill Haven library. The path went near the kiosk, and by unspoken agreement, they stopped to admire the mural. Mia went close to look in the bottom corner.

"It is one of hers," she confirmed, standing back up. "It's even better that the one in the school near the office." She seemed to be studying the whole picture, which showed a happy group of kids, playing on the playground. Then she touched a section where a man was standing in the background, as if he was watching over his child.

The other two watched as she reached out to touch the mural. Noah and Tessa knew of Mia's odd gift, but didn't discuss it. They hadn't really believed it until returning a ring they had found to its owner. Mia had told them who owned it and something private about the owner, who had confirmed it when she had the ring back.

This time, although she frowned, Mia didn't look as distressed as she had the previous evening. She pulled her hand away, and began to walk towards the library.

"Well?" Tessa prompted when she and Noah had caught up. "Anything?"

Mia slowed. "There was a lot of joy there. It's been there a long time though, and lots of people have touched it and left snippets of their own emotions there too. Mostly, they are happy."

"Is that all?" Noah asked, seeing his friend still seemed distant, and frowning faintly.

"Mostly...there was a man in the background, in the shadows... something about him seemed wrong for the picture."

"Okay," Noah said, more to himself. He met a glance from Tessa and decided to keep that comment in mind.

The Library was a quaint building nestled between the town square and a row of charming shops. The library's brick façade was adorned with creeping ivy that whispered the passage of time, and the heavy wooden door creaked as they pushed inside. A musty scent enveloped them, mixed with the faint aroma of old paper and ink.

Mrs. Jenkins, the librarian, was behind the counter, her silver hair pinned neatly in a bun and her glasses perched on the edge of her nose. She looked up as they approached, her expression a mix of curiosity and caution. "Well, if it isn't my favourite trio. What brings you here today, all looking so sombre?"

Noah cleared his throat. "We were hoping to learn more about

Clara. You know, the girl who disappeared a while back?"

Mrs. Jenkins's smile faltered, and for a brief moment, her eyes clouded with something unnameable. "Clara? She was a bright young woman, involved in everything—community events, school plays... She had such a vibrant spirit." Her voice softened, tinged with nostalgia. "But... her disappearance...so soon after her parents... it's a sensitive topic for many in Mill Haven."

Tessa exchanged a glance with Noah and Mia, sensing the weight of the words. "We just want to know what happened. We found her car, and it felt like a sign. Maybe there's something in the records that can help us understand."

Mrs. Jenkins hesitated, her fingers tapping lightly against the wooden counter. "There are some records in the back, but I'm afraid they contain stories that may not be easy to hear. The town has moved on from Clara's disappearance, and some folks hold onto those memories tightly."

"Maybe we can help," Mia said softly, her voice trembling slightly. "We want to make sure she isn't forgotten."

Mrs. Jenkins's gaze softened, and she nodded slowly. "Very well. Follow me."

The trio followed her to a dimly lit storeroom at the back of the library, where shelves bowed under the weight of dusty volumes and boxes filled with photographs and papers. The air felt heavier here, as if the walls themselves held secrets. Mrs. Jenkins checked dates on the boxes, then pulled one from the shelf. The wooden top of an old table creaking as she set it down. "These are some of the records and photographs from ten years ago. You might find something about Clara here."

As they sifted through the contents, some bundled, some loose, a few faded photographs slipped free, fluttering to the floor. One caught Mia's eye—a picture of Clara surrounded by friends, all smiling brightly at the camera. She picked it up, decided it was taken at the outdoor festival. A flicker of emotion washed over her, a brief glimpse into the joy Clara had once felt, but it was tinged with a shadow of sorrow, a whisper of something unresolved.

Tessa pointed at the image. "She looks so happy."

Mia held the photograph gently, her fingers brushing the edges. "But look at her eyes. There's something more there, something hidden." She closed her eyes for a moment, letting the emotions wash over her. "I can feel it. She had a rift with one of her friends. Something changed her."

Noah leaned closer, studying the faces surrounding Clara. "We need to find out who these people are. Maybe they can help us understand what happened." He took out his phone and took a photo of the image.

Tessa lifted a bundle of photos and envelopes. The outer photo caught her attention.

"Here! This looks like a photo of one of those vigils people hold...there's a photo...does that look like Clara to you?"

Noah looked at the photo Tessa held out. "It does. Let's look through that bundle."

They each took a few of the many envelopes, of all different kinds. From amongst them, some dried and faded flower petals fell out. Noah read some quickly, took photos of others. Tessa began to do the same, and when Mia seemed to react to some, took images of those too, even though the contents seemed innocuous.

People from little kids to adults had left letters for Clara, most hoping she was still alive, wishing her to return. The little kids drew pictures, and often had a flower pressed inside. Their message, 'Come back, we love you.' Friends from the local theatre had the message, 'it is not the same with you not here.'

Many notes were signed from the sender, many others were not. Noah found one of those, but he said, "This had to be from Lucas Evans. It's angry, 'you chucked his feelings back in his face, and now he's dead.'"

"Here's one, unsigned, but it says, 'Clara, I'm sorry. I knew you were felling sad. I should have got you to tell me what was wrong. I would have helped you.'" Tessa read. "Did whoever wrote this also know the friend she had a rift with?"

Mia put one down, "That was from one of her father's police colleagues, I think. It says, "I promised your dad to look after you, if anything happened to him. I have let you both down. I won't rest until I know you are safe.' I really feel he meant that. I wonder if he is still working in Mill Haven."

"We can find that out later. Take a picture of that letter," Noah told her.

Mia did that, then after replacing that note in the envelope, reached for another. Several letters later, she pulled one out. The writing was of an older style than kids learnt now. She began to read, but suddenly shook the paper away from her, then tried to rub her fingers on her jeans. "I don't think we should keep looking at these."

Noah took the letter and photographed it. "I doubt we will learn much more here," he said.

As they collected the separate piles of photos and envelopes to put back in the box, they found a group of photos. "These were taken at the vigil, of the people there. I didn't see any of these in the paper," Noah told the two girls. He quickly snapped photos of each one in the pile.

They repacked the box as murmurs from the main area of the library reached them. The indistinguishable snippets of conversation had a tone that felt urgent and charged. Tessa glanced toward the door, her expression shifting. "We're not the only ones interested in Clara's story. I can feel it."

Suddenly, the door swung open, and several elderly townsfolk shuffled in, their eyes scanning the library the shelves in the storage room with a mix of nostalgia and wariness. The group's chatter about past festivals faded, and an uneasy silence settled over them as they noticed the trio.

Noah's heart raced as he caught their wary glances, the tension thickening the air around them. "Maybe we should go," he suggested quietly, but Mia shook her head.

"No. We can't run from this. Not now."

Mia's determination spurred them forward as she turned back to Mrs. Jenkins who had followed the other townsfolk into the room. "Do you have any other records or stories about Clara? Anything that might explain what happened?"

Tessa quickly added, "There was nothing useful there."

Mrs. Jenkins sighed, her features softening once more. "There are some tales that are best left undisturbed, dear. But if it's the truth you seek, you might find it in the old community hall. Clara often volunteered there, and the records might still be kept."

The elderly townsfolk began to approach, their expressions unreadable but their intent clear. Noah felt the weight of their eyes on him, the pressure building as he glanced back at Mia and Tessa, who stood resolute beside him.

"Thank you, Mrs. Jenkins," Tessa said, her voice steady despite the tension. "We'll go there next."

As they made their way back toward the main room, Noah slipped his phone back into his pocket. He didn't need to look to know those townsfolk were staring after them. Mia's rigid posture confirmed the feeling. The whispers that followed them. The trio stepped out into the sunlight, the warmth washing over them as they left the shadows of the library behind.

In the bustling town square, the local festival was underway, vibrant colours stretching across stalls filled with homemade crafts, baked goods, and laughter. The cheerful atmosphere felt like a stark contrast to the heaviness they had just experienced. But before they could fully embrace the festivities, a figure caught their attention, an elderly woman standing alone, her gaze fixed on them.

"Mia?" the woman called out, her voice trembling with emotion. "Mia Chang?"

Mia hesitated, her heart racing as she recognized the woman as one of her grandmother's friends. The warmth of the festival faded, and an unspoken tension filled the space between them. The woman's eyes flared with recognition and concern, but her expression shifted, a guarded look crossing her features as she shuffled closer.

"Please," she said, her tone urgent but soft. "Leave Clara's story alone. Some things are better buried."

Mia felt a chill race down her spine, the woman's warning echoing in her mind. "But we need to know what happened to her. It's important."

The woman shook her head, her voice sharp yet laced with sorrow. "You don't understand. The past is a dangerous place. You don't want to stir those waters."

Before Mia could respond, the woman turned and melted back

into the crowd, leaving them with a sense of foreboding.

Noah glanced at Mia and Tessa, the uncertainty palpable between them.

"Who was that?" Noah asked.

"Grandma's friend Lucy Yuan. I always thought her odd. She once told my dad, not to go walking near the creek, which he used to do a lot. That was just before an unexpected cloud burst, which flooded that track and washed away the foot bridge."

"I'm starting to agree with that old woman," Tessa said quietly.

"What do we do now?" Noah asked, his voice a hushed murmur. A message pinged to his phone, but the recent warning was too ominous to think of it.

Mia clutched a photograph of Clara she'd taken from the library box. There had been two copies. Her resolve hardened, in spite of the warning. He grandma had once told her, she would know when something needed doing. "We keep going. We owe it to her."

Their determination surged as they made their way through the bustling square, the festival's laughter ringing hollow against the weight of their task. As they reached the edge of the crowd, a shadow flickered at the corner of Noah's eye—an unfamiliar figure watching them from a distance, cloaked in the shadows of a nearby stall.

"Mia," he whispered, his voice barely audible. "Do you see that person? Over near the pony ride stall?"

Mia turned, her heart racing as she caught sight of the figure, the sense of being watched creeping over her like a chill. "Yes. Who are they?"

Tessa's expression shifted, her protective instincts flaring. Noah had only seen one person. Mia had sensed there were more. "We need to be careful. This is getting serious."

Noah took a deep breath, glancing back at the festival, the vibrant colours now feeling like a facade over the brewing storm. "Let's head to the community hall. We have to find out what's really going on."

As he began walking, he checked the message. Then he stopped abruptly. "Let's head back to my place instead."

"Why?" Mia asked.

Noah handed her his phone so she could read the message. She did, aloud, so Tessa could hear.

"I'm really sorry, lad, those people didn't like me helping you. I had to make them think I was misdirecting you. There is nothing at the hall. There is a painting here of hers, from a display. It was never picked up."

With renewed determination, they stepped away from the laughter, the weight of Clara's story pressing heavily on their hearts, a mystery that beckoned them forward into the shadows of Mill Haven's past.

Chapter 3: The First Vision

The delicious scent of homemade bread lingered in the kitchen where Noah had invited then to sit. The old metal framed Formica table held a scattering of pictures Noah had printed from his phone. Mia added the photo she had taken from Mill Haven library. The one with Clara prominently in the picture. Tessa was in the process of connecting her phone to the printer. As the printer ejected Tessa's photos, Noah raised the kitchen blinds further, and opened the window to let a light breeze in.

Outside, the breeze carried sounds from the festival, several streets away. Laughter and squeals of delight, carrying the clearest. Closer to hand, cicadas tried out their own music. Inside, an air of tension hung over the trio like storm clouds.

"Let's look at what we got," Noah suggested, as Mia caught a sheet of paper about to waft onto the floor.

Tessa began, "Half the town must have gone to that vigil for Clara. All the kids from the child care centre, the people in the theatre group, her art students, heaps of shop keepers. Nearly all had nice things to say, and wanted her to come back."

"They weren't all like that," Noah told her.

"No, there were a few odd ones." She scrolled through the photos on her phone to find the ones she'd copied. She re-read the one from the unnamed friend, who regretted not finding out what Clara had been hiding. "How can we find out who this was from? It's unsigned."

"Maybe if we look in the school yearbooks," Mia proposed. "It sounds like that person was a really close friend."

"We could start there," Tessa agreed. "I might be able to find out. I'm on the yearbook committee this year. We get to look at old issues to get ideas."

"And that one, I thought was from one of her father's police friends," Mia recalled. "There was a name there, Tom Nicholls. Can we find out if he's still working?"

"I might ask my mum," Noah thought. "She sometimes delivers coffee to the police station. I know she's friendly with a few of the guys there."

"Was that before or after you were picked up with Cory West?" Tessa teased.

Noah's face reddened at the memory. "How was I to know he'd pinched the car? He said it had been kept in his dad's garage for years. He wanted to see if I thought it worth fixing up." To change the topic, he asked, "What was in that last one you looked at Mia?"

"I didn't read more than Dear Clara."

"What did you feel?" Tessa asked, gently.

"Like I was suffocating," Mia admitted.

"Let me print that one out," Noah suggested. His printer spat out a sheet and he went to get it. He began to decipher the old style writing.

"Read it out," Tessa suggested.

"Dear Clara, you are a beautiful spirit, full of potential, full of secrets, safe in God's hands," Noah read. "It sounds like the writer thinks she's dead, doesn't it? Was that what you sensed, Mia?"

"Not then, but..." she went silent, recalling the emotions that had caused her to throw that letter away. "No, I didn't get that. I think I got the suffocating feeling from Clara, but I think she was with the person who wrote the letter, and that person terrified her, and was somehow smug because he had her, and no one knew."

"That's scary," Tessa admitted, feeling a chill at the thought of Clara a prisoner. "Do you think that means she might still be alive?"

"It's been ten years," Noah pointed out. "That writing suggests someone old. Older than mum's generation. Maybe the way it was written is due to the generation."

"Or one of those crazy old guys who walk through town preaching the gospel to us heathens," Tessa recalled. "My mother used to threaten to set the police on them for accosting people and preaching without a permit."

"We can keep those ideas in our heads," Noah suggested. "I read the letter Lucas Evans wrote. I reckon it was grief talking, because he accused Clara of walking all over his brother's feelings, and using him for her own reasons. Lucas idolised his brother."

"He might have heard the argument," Mia suggested. "Could we talk to him?"

Noah considered that. Lucas worked at the garage where Noah worked after school and some weekends.

Mia began to tidy up the printed images, and she froze when a tingle ran from her fingers to her spine. "We have the pictures from the vigil. They must have been taken by the photographer from the paper. I wonder if we can recognise anyone who was there and talk to them."

"Something to think about," Noah said cautiously. He was recalling the older folk at the library. "Though if people don't want us to stir things up, asking questions would show them we were. In any case, the police probably questioned any one that knew Clara. So if they learnt nothing, we probably won't either."

"Well, let's see if we do recognise anyone, and add their name to a list," Tessa suggested, taking her phone out to do just that.

One photo Noah recognised as being from the local paper. He went back to the paper's archive site to check. He was able to get the names of a group of smiling girls from the caption. Clara was in the image, right at the centre, with others from her theatre group. It had been taken at the party after the end of the play, "Oklahoma". They'd kept to the theme of the show and had the party outside in the hobby farm at the end of town.

"Rachel Jacobs?" Tessa repeated one of the names. "I think that's Cassie's older sister."

"And Todd Rafferty, was just a few years ahead of us at school," Noah recalled. "The rest of the names mean nothing to me. But add them to the list anyway. Hand over another picture."

Mia obliged. "No one looks familiar to me, but I didn't live here back then."

As her two friends scanned the second picture, heads almost touching as they tried to pick up details, Mia grabbed a third picture.

Her eyes fell immediately on an older man, out of place amongst the crowd who knew Clara well. Then she realised, he wasn't the only older person there – she recognised some of the shop keepers in town. Still, that man stood out for wearing an expensive looking suit, while the other adults were dressed casually, or like they had come from work. A familiar tingle brushed her neck, and a recollection of the mural on the kiosk came to her. She'd seen it so often, she knew the details by heart, yet somehow, the image of the well-dressed man at the vigil, superimposed itself over the shadowy man she had noticed when she'd passed the kiosk that morning. She tried to recall if she had a picture of the kiosk on her phone, or downloaded it to her computer.

"Mia?" Tessa nudged her. "Anything in that one?"

"Some shop people, a man in a suit," she summarised, not sure what to make of the odd fancy she'd had. "Do either of you have a picture of that mural on the kiosk?"

Noah shook his head, Tessa said, "No, why?"

"Probably nothing. Just an odd notion with nothing to back it up. Though I'd like to see more of Clara's work. It really is good. Do you know of any others besides that and the one at school?"

"That one Ms Jenkins mentioned in the text," Noah reminded her. "We can go back to the library tomorrow. Say we left something there when we were going through old festival photos or something."

Noah leaned back in his chair, his hazel eyes darting between Mia and Tessa, gauging their reactions. "So, what do you think? I mean, we've been at this for ages. I don't think there's much more we can extract from what we have so far." His voice was low, almost lost beneath the soft rustle of pages, but it carried a weight that drew his friends' attention back to the task at hand.

"I think we're still missing a lot of pieces of the puzzle," Tessa replied, her green eyes narrowing as she scrutinized a photograph of Clara, a girl with bright laughter captured in a moment now lost to time. "Those articles in the paper mention her argument with someone, but they don't say who. It's like she quickly faded from everyone's memory."

Mia, perched on the edge of her seat, traced her fingers over the photograph she had taken from the library, her heart thrumming against her ribcage. "Maybe we need to dig deeper," she suggested, her voice trembling slightly. "What if... what if I try to connect with the photograph? You know, like before?"

Noah's expression shifted, a flicker of concern shadowing his features. "Do you think that's a good idea? What if it's too much?"

She met his gaze, a mix of determination and anxiety swirling in her almond-shaped eyes. "I have to try. Clara deserves to be heard."

Tessa nodded in agreement, her protective instincts flaring. "Just be careful, okay? We don't know what kind of emotions are tied to that picture."

As Mia held the photo and thought of only Clara, and the smiling face in the photo, she closed her eyes. The world around her faded, and a new one emerged, vibrant and chaotic. She felt the familiar pull at the edges of her consciousness, the flickering memories washing over her like waves crashing against the shore. The scent of gasoline mingled with the sharp tang of metal, and suddenly, she was there, standing in a sun-drenched field beside the abandoned car, no longer a wreck.

Her heart raced as she saw Clara, her now familiar dark hair catching a ghostly light, her face painted with frustration. "You don't understand!" Clara's voice echoed in Mia's mind, laced with an urgency that made her breath hitch. "I can't just pretend everything's fine! Not anymore! We have to tell the police."

A dark shadowy shape looming nearer. "It's you who don't understand! Anyone who talks about them...things happen to them. Look at your folks, do you want to end up like them? Your dad was an excellent cop, he did all that advanced training, for when he was doing pursuits. Do you think it likely he just drove off the road, at that very point, to end up down here? Like we did."

"That car forced you off," Clara insisted. "If you hadn't had that drink—"

"One beer, that's all I had. I am not drunk. We need to leave here before they realise we didn't die."

"How will we explain the car being here?"

"I'll tell them I'd had more drinks. I'd rather take the rap for that than mention them."

"Okay, I'll get my bag. Do you have a torch in the car?"

"No. There's enough moonlight. We need to hurry."

The shadowy shape moved back, and the image morphed into an image of sky, and a tree in silhouette. Hands, gripping rocks to help with the climb, and a sense of terror, caused by flashing torches below. Reaching the road, hearing voices, pushing something into a hole between tree roots, then...

Mia's hands clenched as she watched Clara argue with a figure obscured by shadow—a friend, perhaps, or something more. She strained to hear the words, to understand the glimpse of the emotions swirling between them, but they slipped away like grains of sand. The tension was palpable, and she felt it gnaw at her chest, a reflection of Clara's own turmoil.

"Mia!" Tessa's voice broke through the haze, yanking her back to the present. Noah's kitchen with its wooden shelves and the afternoon sunlight through the window broke the terror, but the heaviness of Clara's emotions lingered, a ghostly echo in her heart.

Mia gasped, her chest heaving as she shook off the remnants of the vision. "Clara... she was upset. There was someone she was arguing with, but I couldn't see who it was."

Noah leaned closer, his brow furrowed. "What were they arguing about?"

"I-I don't know," Mia stammered, her voice still trembling. "But it felt... it felt important. Clara was desperate, like she was fighting for something she believed in, something that mattered to her." Mia drew a breath and concentrated on the vivid seeing, relating what she recalled.

Tessa leaned back, her expression thoughtful. "This changes everything. If Clara knew of someone's secret, something she thought the police should know, it could explain why she is missing. Maybe she had told her father something."

As they processed this revelation, a sudden chill seemed to sweep through the kitchen, causing Tessa to shiver. "I don't like this," she muttered, her voice low. "Something feels off about all of this."

Before anyone could respond, Tessa's eyes widened, and she grabbed Noah's arm, her grip firm and urgent. "Noah! I saw someone... a shadow ducking past the window."

"What do you mean?" Noah asked, his voice steady despite the rising tension. He hurried to look out into his backyard as she answered.

"I don't know, it's just a feeling," Tessa admitted, her brows knitted in concentration, watching him scan his backyard. "But it's dangerous. We have to be careful. Whatever's happening, it's not just about Clara. There's something else lurking in the shadows. Something way bigger."

Mia's heart raced at Tessa's words, a knot of anxiety tightening in her stomach. "You think someone is watching us now?"

"They're gone, I think," Tessa replied, her voice barely above a whisper. "But we can't ignore the possibility. We have to keep our eyes open."

The three friends fell into a heavy silence, the weight of their discoveries settling around them like a thick fog. Noah's protective instincts surged to the forefront, and he ran a hand through his tousled hair, frustration mingling with concern. "We can't let fear control us, but we also can't rush in blindly," he said, his tone firm. "We need to figure out what we're facing before we go back to that field."

Mia's heart sank as she glanced at Tessa, who looked equally uncertain. "But we can't just stop searching for Clara. We owe it to her to understand what happened."

"I know," Noah replied, his voice softening. "But we need a plan. We can't let emotions cloud our judgment."

Tessa nodded, her expression resolute. "Let's regroup, go over everything we have found out so far, and decide our next steps carefully. We're stronger together, and we can do this if we're smart about it."

Mia felt a flicker of hope at Tessa's words, and she straightened, brushing back her hair and taking a deep breath. "Okay. We'll figure this out. Together."

As they gathered the printed pages and notes, the air around them felt charged with a new determination. The sun was beginning to dip lower in the sky, casting long shadows into the kitchen window. With every picture and note they tucked away, they were weaving a tapestry of Clara's story, one thread at a time.

"Before we leave," Noah said, glancing at the neat pile of print outs on the table, "Let's make sure we are all clear about what we need to do and what we will do next."

Mia's fingers flicked through the articles and notes, her mind racing with possibilities.

Noah began. "I'll sound out mum about the old policeman, and if she knows where he is now. And next time I'm at work, I might see if Clarrie will tell me anymore."

"I'll check out old year books, on Monday if I can," Tessa decided. "The group meet then."

"I've got art group Monday evening too, I can find out if Ms Dewar knows about Clara, or the picture at school. I want to get another picture of the kiosk mural too."

"You might be able to do that tomorrow," Noah suggested. "But I was thinking, the library doesn't open until ten tomorrow. What say we go back to that field early? Sun gets up about seven, what say we aim to be there then?"

"Okay," Tessa agreed. Mia nodded.

"When we get back, we can get breakfast in town, and check out the festival until the library opens," Noah finished. Both girls nodded.

"I'd better head home," Mia announced.

"Me too," Tessa agreed.

"I'll walk back with you," Noah told them. "Mum should be finishing up soon. I'll try to meet up with her."

It was still two hours off sunset, but at that time of the year, the sun went behind the hills, sending the hills shadow over the town. Already the carnival lights were coming on drawing in the late arriving patrons.

Mia suddenly gasped, and pointed. "There! That shadow... it's watching us."

Noah squinted into the growing darkness. "I can't see anyone."

Tessa's eyes widened as she scanned the area. "We need to go. Now."

Noah trusted Tessa's hunches as much as he had come to accept Mia's odd ability.

With a sudden urgency, they hurried down the path, their footsteps echoing in the stillness of the evening. The shadow lingered just out of sight, a reminder of the dangers lurking in the depths of their investigation.

Noah was relieved when first Mia, then Tessa arrived home and went inside. He'd pressed a roll of photocopied sheets into her hand at the last minute. He kept going to the café where his mother was working, keeping his eyes scanning the road around him.

Chapter 4: A Ghost from the Past

The rusty old car sat like a sentinel in the abandoned field, its surface dulled by fire and years of neglect, the rust patches giving it a mottled appearance. Noah, Mia, and Tessa gathered on the edge of the road, looking down into the bowl called Parson's Folly. Their breath visible in the chill of the early morning. As the sun slowly rose in the sky, long shadows clawed at the ground, stretching across the wild grass, which swayed gently in a breeze that whispered secrets of the past. It was an eerie scene, one that made Mia shiver, her gaze darting nervously toward the skeletal trees lining the far edge of the field.

"I don't like this place," she murmured, tucking a strand of hair behind her ear, her dark eyes clouded with apprehension. "I didn't notice it before, but it feels... haunted."

Noah turned to her, his hazel eyes warm with reassurance. "It's just an old car, Mia. Clara's story is out there, and we need to find it. Let's see what's here. Where do you think she hid her bag?"

Tessa, arms crossed and leaning against the tall sentinel tree, squinted across the expanse of the bowl, her green eyes scanning the tree line. "Yeah, but what if we're digging too deep? The few people who know we are looking into Clara seem reluctant to talk about her. Maybe there's a reason for that."

The tension in the air thickened, a palpable sense of unease settling over them. Noah's gaze flickered to Tessa, the weight of her words hanging heavily in the air. He could feel her protective instincts kicking in, a quality he admired but also found frustrating. "We can't back down now. We all agree, Clara deserves to have her story told," he insisted, his voice steady but laced with an undercurrent of anxiety.

Mia stepped closer to the tree, her fingers brushing against the rough texture, and a wave of energy surged through her. She closed her eyes, letting the remnants of Clara's spirit seep into her consciousness. Flickers of laughter, sunlight filtering through leaves, and the warmth of friendship enveloped her, but it was immediately followed by a cold rush of fear and darkness, the need to hide something. She gasped, pulling her hand away as though burned.

"Noah, I saw something," she said, her voice trembling. "Clara was happy coming here once, but... there's something else. Something dark."

Tessa's brows knitted together, her instinct to shield her friends from harm clashing with an unquenchable curiosity. "What do you mean dark? Are you sure?"

Before Mia could respond, Noah's attention snapped to the tree line, where shadows danced between the trunks. A figure, cloaked and hooded, stood partially obscured by the branches. The sight sent a jolt of adrenaline through his veins. "Look!" he whispered urgently, pointing.

Mia's breath caught in her throat, and Tessa's eyes widened, darting to the spot Noah indicated. The figure seemed to watch them, unmoving, a ghostly presence that made the hairs on the back of Mia's neck stand on end. "Do you think it's someone from town?" she whispered, her voice barely audible.

Noah squinted, trying to discern the figure's features. "We need to find out who it is. We can't just let this go."

"You want to confront a stranger lurking in the woods?" Tessa's tone was incredulous, but beneath it was a flicker of fear mixed with excitement. "What if they're dangerous?"

"We can't back down now," Noah insisted again, determination hardening his resolve. "Let's see if they know anything about Clara."

Mia hesitated, glancing back at the figure, which seemed to shift slightly, as if aware of their gaze. "What if it's not just a person? What if it's... something else?"

Noah took a deep breath, his heart racing. "We won't know until we get closer. We have to stick together, okay?"

With reluctant nods, the trio found the track down to the bowl, and moved toward the woods, each step crunching softly over twigs and leaves.

In the trees, the underbrush was thick, the familiar sounds of nature muted in the shadows. The atmosphere shifted, an unsettling quiet replacing the rustle of grass and the calls of distant birds. Mia felt a chill run through her, not just from fear, but from an inexplicable sense that they were crossing into a different realm, one filled with secrets and shadows.

As they reached the edge of the trees, the figure had disappeared into the darkness. Noah cursed under his breath, glancing around for any sign of movement. "Where did he go?" he asked, frustration seeping into his voice.

Tessa pushed forward, more cautious than before. "Maybe they're just hiding. We should—"

Her words were cut off by the sight of an old campsite nestled between the trees—a charred fire pit surrounded by a ring of stones, remnants of a life, long abandoned. Scattered belongings, lay torn and filthy on the ground, a tattered blanket, a corroded billy, and a strip of flimsy cloth, caught on a prickly bush and fluttering slightly in the breeze.

Mia approached the remnants, her heart racing with a mix of trepidation and curiosity. She bent down to touch the cloth strip, feeling a pulse of energy surge through her fingertips. Images flooded her mind—Clara laughing with a friend, sunlight filtering through the leaves as they shared a picnic rug, a warmth that felt like home. Then the vision twisted into something darker: shadows creeping closer, a scream, the sensation of being lost.

She jerked back, breathless, and stumbled into Tessa, who steadied her. "Mia! What did you see?" Tessa's voice was sharp with concern.

"I don't know," Mia panted, her voice quaking. "It was... it saw Clara, but something happened here. Something bad."

Noah knelt beside her, his brow furrowed. "If Clara was here, then maybe she was connected to whoever that figure was. We have to find out what happened."

Mia straightened, and walked to touch the billy. An inanimate object should have less emotional residue, and it might give her a hint of the other person with Clara. As quickly as she touched it, she dragged her finger away. Even that brief and tentative touch almost overwhelmed her with its vileness. She whimpered. She couldn't speak.

Tessa glanced back toward the trees, unease etching deeper lines into her face. She answered Noah's comment. "But what if we're not supposed to? What if we are digging into things that shouldn't be unearthed?"

A crack echoed through the woods, a sharp snap of a branch that sent a jolt through the trio. They turned in unison, hearts pounding in their chests, to see a shadowy figure emerging from the trees stopping within conversational distance. There was no way of knowing if it was the same man they had seen before.

This figure had muscles straining the sleeves of a mottled green, long sleeved tee-shirt, and his face was half obscured by the hood of a sleeveless vest of brown homespun fabric. His hands, dangling down his sides were, like the skin of his neck, a weathered brown. Tendrils of dirty blond hair escaped the hood, framing his face. His lower face sported a roughly trimmed beard, but the jaw was strong, suggesting he was young, maybe in his late twenties.

His gaze burned with a frightening intensity, but at the same time seemed to have a haunted expression, hinting at a troubled life.

"Stay away from here," he warned, his voice low and gravelly, filled with an urgency that made the hairs on the back of Mia's neck stand on end. "This land is cursed – no good comes from being here."

Noah stepped forward, instinctively protective and defiant. "Who are you? Do you know Clara? We know she was here."

The man's eyes narrowed, weighing them with a grave intensity. "I knew Clara. She shouldn't have come here. None of you should be here."

"Why?" Tessa pressed, her voice steady despite the tension crackling in the air. "What do you know about her? About what happened?"

A strained silence stretched between them, the man's haunted gaze flickering to the car before returning to the trio. "There are things in this town that people don't talk about. Secrets that are better left buried. Clara... she was drawn to them." He paused, the weight of unspoken truths heavy in the air. "If you care about her, you need to leave. Now."

Mia stepped forward, propelled by an instinct she could hardly understand. She reached out a hand as if pleading, managing to touch his before he jerked it away. "You can't just leave us with this. We need to know what happened to her. We can't walk away."

The man's expression shifted slightly, a flicker of something—regret?—crossing his face. "You don't understand what you're asking. The past isn't something you can just uncover. It has a way of consuming you."

Tessa felt a surge of unease wash over her, and her foresight kicked in, images flashing through her mind: danger, shadows closing in, and a sense of urgency that made her heart race. "We should go," she urged, glancing at Noah and Mia. "He's right. This place isn't safe."

"No," Noah said firmly, his resolve hardening. "We're not leaving until we get answers."

The man's mouth tightened, his jaw set in a grim line. "Damn it Bennett, listen to me. If you stay, danger will find you. You'll find things you're not ready to face."

Mia felt a surge of compassion mingled with fear. "But Clara deserves to be remembered. We can't let her story fade away."

The man hesitated, the conflict in his gaze evident. He seemed to weigh their resolve against the danger that loomed in the shadows. "You're brave, but bravery can be foolish," he finally said. Then his voice dropped to a near whisper. "The truth isn't always what you expect. Sometimes it's more terrifying than you can imagine."

With that, he turned and retreated into the woods, moving more quietly than he had arrived, his figure swallowed by the shadowy darkness. Silence enveloped the trio, leaving only the sound of their ragged breaths and the rustle of leaves in the fading light.

Noah felt a chill run down his spine, his heart racing as the weight of the man's warning settled over them like a shroud. "What do we do now?" he asked, looking between Mia and Tessa.

Tessa's expression was resolute, a mix of concern and determination. "We leave here and regroup. We need to talk about what we just heard. But I'm with you, Mia. I know Clara's story matters, and we can't just leave it behind.

Mia nodded, her heart pounding with a mix of fear and urgency.

"I feel like we're close. I need to go back to the car. There's something there waiting for us."

That was a flash of what she had received from the figure. He'd seen them here before, hoped they would come back, had hidden something there.

As they turned back toward the field, the sun was now noticeably higher, painting the sky a deep azure blue. The day's brightness was incongruous when the air seemed thick with a sense of foreboding. The ghost of Clara's past loomed large, and as they approached the car, Mia felt the weight of unspoken truths pressing in around them.

Some instinct was drawing her to the passenger side door – propped eternally in a half open position. She crouched down to reach in under the seat, and Noah stood where any observers could not see what she was doing.

"I'd really love to be able to do this wreck up," he said aloud. "These used to be great cars, capable of more than you'd think just looking at them."

Tessa seemed to intuit what he was doing, and told him, "Typical males. All they want to talk about is cars, preferable fast cars. I can run faster than this thing."

"Funny, Tess. I could remind you about always talking sport!"

They continued the mock argument while Mia drew a 6 inch long, inch wide, sealed metal tube from where she'd put her hand. Noah turned to look into the car, while his hand grabbed the tube. He managed to slip it into a pocket, then moved so Mia could get up.

"That wasn't what I expected," Mia told him. "But we still have to find her bag."

"You said you saw her shove it in a hole, near the tree?" Noah asked her to confirm.

"Yes, to the left of the tree. I can't see a hole from here."

Noah scanned the area, didn't see anyone near there watching. But he hadn't forgotten how the apparition in the trees had known his name. "The track we took is on the other side of the tree, and it's not as steep. You girls take that way, I'm going to rock climb it. When I get near the top, I'll make like I need help up the last bit of the way. Don't act too smart. I will need a bit of time to see if I can find the hole.”

He went slowly, deliberately, to let the girls get up there first. He was watching the hand and foot holds, as well as the places where creatures had burrowed into the steep cliff. He let out a yell when a fox darted out in front of him with a wriggling rabbit in his mouth.

“You afraid of a fox and a dead rabbit,” Tessa called down, teasing him as if she had nothing more important on her mind.

Noah called up, “Why don’t you come down here and try to climb over rabbit shit.”

“You had to be so smart,” Tessa called down. Her voice seemed to echo across the bowl.

Mia was watching intently as Noah put a tentative hand in the hole and began to feel around. “Be careful,” she urged.

Noah hardly heard her, for his hand had found something that felt like soft leather. He gently yanked on it, and drew it out. Tessa lay on the ground, holding her hand down as if to take his hand and help him up. Mia couched down and took the top of the drawstring bag from him and slid it into her own carry bag. She tried not to think of the mess that adorned it.

Noah finished the climb up, it hadn’t been hard, he’d just made it look that way. He looked back down, then across the bowl. If anyone was watching them, they stayed hidden. At least the road, as far as they could see each side of the bend, had no one in sight.

“Let’s get going,” Noah urged. Neither Tessa nor Mia needed telling twice. Their quest was far from over, and the way forward far from certain, and they were not ready to confront the cause of the darkness Mia had seen. Not yet.

Chapter 5 - Shadows

They stopped before they reached the town, moving off the road where a huge tree had been cut down, but not yet removed. It provided some cover from the occasional passing car, and a place to look at what they had found.

Noah took out the metal tube, for a better look. It had a screw lid, but it wouldn't open. Closer inspection suggested heat had been applied to the screw area. The tube itself was plain silver, like some he'd seen with dissolving energy tablets.

"We'll have to try to get this open," Noah announced, before replacing it in his pocket.

Mia took the dirty leather drawstring bag from her shoulder bag and shook a lot of dirt and fur off it. In the sunlight, the leather once light brown, looked stained.

"I used to want a bag like that," Tessa admitted. "Someone used to make them to sell at the festival and craft market days."

Mia seemed reluctant to open the bag. Noah asked, "You picking up something?"

"No..."

"Here, give it to me," Tessa offered.

"No, I'll do it," Mia decided. Her slender fingers eased open the drawstrings, so she could reach into it. Nothing felt important, so she upended the bag on the tree log and let things fall out. Deodorant, hair brush, tampons, spare car keys, a perfume stick, two pens and a palm sized notebook – the sort of stuff women carried.

Tessa pounced on the book, flipped through a few pages, and put it down.

"I don't understand," Mia murmured. "I was sure there was something in here."

"There's no ID, driver's licence, ATM cards or phone," Noah pointed out.

"She probably took those with her," Tessa said, impatiently. "Are there any zipped pockets, or another section? An unstitched part of the lining?" She watched as Mia examined the inside.

"Here!" Mia exclaimed. There was a slit under a part if the drawstring seam, like a coin pocket. She put a finger into it and touched a couple of keys. With a bit of fiddling, they came out. They all just stared.

"One looks like a house key, but I've not seen anything like that other one," Noah admitted, scratching his head.

"Nor me," Tessa agreed.

"I may have," Mia said thoughtfully. "I'm just not sure where. Was there anything in the notebook?"

Tessa passed it to her, and watched her friend's face as she looked through the pages. The writing was cryptic, initials for people of places. On the last page with writing, she touched the writing. "She was leaving. Going somewhere, this as an address. Meeting someone."

"That fits with what you got at the car," Noah pointed out. "But that doesn't help us. Unless you got something on who she was meeting?"

"No," Mia shook her head.

"What now?" Tessa asked.

"Put everything but the keys and the notebook back in the bag. There might not be anything of use there, but I don't think we should just dump it."

A car swept past on the road, as he spoke. He thought to himself, if someone spotted them here, that knew where they had just come from, and they left the bag here, they would have proof we found something.

It seemed Tessa either read his mind or had the same idea. "You're right. That man certainly didn't want us poking around there."

"I'll put the notebook in my bag," Mia said.

"I'll put the keys on with my house and locker keys," Tessa decided. "Hide them in plain sight."

"Great ideas. We should make sure all our notes and stuff we find are kept safe."

"Was that why you gave me the stuff from last night?" Tessa asked.

"Yeah. After we saw that shadow at the window, I didn't want to keep it there," Noah admitted.

"I think we should record all we find, and sense from things and places," Tessa said, once they were back walking along the road.

"Even when and where we feel things," Noah agreed. "You okay to do that, Mia?"

"I have been. It's something my gran said I should do."

They continued in silence, glad the road was rarely used, but feeling exposed when one did. "I wonder why Clara hid her bag," Tessa said, revealing what she had been thinking of. "I can't see anything in the notebook being dangerous, and one key was probably her house key."

"What if it wasn't?" Noah asked idly.

"HUH?" Tessa blurted.

"What if she wasn't going to stay away for good, and intended to come back. Wouldn't she take her house key with her?"

"Probably, I guess," Tessa had to agree.

"She felt she was being followed, and they were intending to get her," Mia recalled the vision. "Anyone could find out where she lived if they didn't already know, and if they wanted to get in they would. Leaving the key hidden wouldn't have made any difference. Unless, it fits a hidden lock."

"Hidden where?" Noah asked. "That's the question."

The girls nodded agreement.

During the hour they still had to wait for the library to open, Noah, Tessa and Mia strolled around the festival as the stalls reopened and the other activities got underway. They acted like any of their classmates would, except they all glanced around, wondering if they were being watched.

Nearer ten, they moved to where they could watch the library entrance, and as soon as they saw the big wooden outer doors open, they left their seats and wandered over.

"Goodness, you three are keen," Lina Castle, the duty librarian commented. "I wasn't expecting to see anyone today, with the festival and all."

"Oh, we're intending to get back there," Noah grinned.

"So, can I help you I some way?"

Mia spoke up, "Actually, I came to ask if I could look for something in the store room. Ms Jenkins let us look through a box of miscellaneous photos taken at local events. That was yesterday. But I can't find my art pencils. I think I might have lost them in there. I need them for art tomorrow."

Lina frowned a moment, then nodded. "I'll let you in for a quick look. You won't be looking in boxes today, will you?"

"As interesting as it was, I have other plans for today," Mia said looking directly at her.

After the door was open, Tessa and Noah wondered how to distract the librarian, so she didn't hover. However, as luck would have it, movement out near the front desk caught her attention and she hurried off. Noah ducked into the room to help Mia look for the picture Ms Jenkins had mentioned. Tessa stood guard outside.

Noah and Mia had just emerged when Lina returned. Mia had her box of pencils in her hand and looked to be trying to put them back in her bag.

"Where ever were you poking around?" Lina exclaimed, seeing the dust on Noah's sleeve.

"Under one of the shelves," Noah said, brushing at his sleeve. It had actually come from getting the framed picture out from behind one of the storage racks.

"My pencils were there. They must have fallen out and got kicked," Mia shrugged. "I'm glad I found them though. I didn't want to ask my mum for a new set already."

"All's well then. Go off and enjoy the festival."

They wandered around, each buying one or two things from various stalls before they headed to get doughnuts and milkshakes to eat at one of the set up tables.

"It was there," Tessa finally asked. Mia nodded.

"The light wasn't good, but it was definitely one of Clara's pictures. Looked like it was of the corner of the park near the shops, where the interstate buses stop," Mia gave her opinion. "It looks different to what I recall, though."

"How?" Tessa asked.

"I'd need to swing by there to look," Mia decided. "Things might have changed between when I was last around there and when the painting was done."

Noah's phone rang. He answered it and turned around to speak. "Hello Mr Westbrook. Yes, I can come straight from school. Alright." Still considering the call, Noah looked up and for a moment saw a shadow duck behind the refreshment stall.

"Let's go back to my place," Noah invited the others.

"What's up?" Mia asked.

"We are still being watched," Noah told them. "It makes no sense, really. All we did was go see the old car, then to the library. Why follow us around?"

"Maybe Ms Jenkins mentioned what we were doing?" Mia suggested.

"No," Tessa disagreed. "Those old people who came in must have heard something. Noah has a point though. There has to be more about that car, and surely we aren't the only kids who go out there. Hey! That creepy guy today, he knew you by name. Do you know him?"

"I didn't recognise him," Noah admitted. "I'll have to think about that."

"I've just thought of something," Mia said. "You know, sometimes what I see isn't easy to understand, but when I first touched the car, I saw the driver slumped over the wheel, blood on his face. And Clara, out of the car. When I used the photo last night, both Kaelen and Clara were alive – uninjured. They climbed up the hill to where Clara hid her bag."

"Whoa!" Tessa exhaled. "The papers all said the crash down from the road killed Kaelen. If they did an autopsy, obviously the result didn't change that idea."

"No one saw anything of Clara after that day. It was her car, so they would have tried to find her. And from what you saw, Mia, she was there with him," Noah summed up. "Whatever happened to her, happened there. It had to be. If so, what do those shadowy people think we might find?"

None of the three had any ideas they wanted to share. All the possibilities they thought of were unpleasant.

"I'd like to know who those people are," Tessa said, with a shiver. "They are the ones hiding secrets."

"But how to find out who they are without word getting back about it," Noah stated their fear. "I'd say, we leave them alone for now, while we see if we can figure out Clara's story."

"I do want to find more of her pictures, surely she did a lot. I did a quick search on her, and found a site where she sold cards and pictures with her work," Mia said.

"Is it still operating?" Tessa asked with sudden intensity.

"I...don't know. I assumed I reached a cached page."

"I wouldn't try looking there further," Noah warned. "These days, people can figure out where people who visit a site, come from."

They arrived at Noah's house, and like last time, went around the back to enter.

Tessa grabbed his arm to stop him going to the door. "Did you leave the door open?"

"Shit!" Noah swore. They all listened, but heard no noises coming from the house. "Stay out here," he told the girls before going cautiously inside. A short time later he came back out.

"There's no one there now. I reckon someone has been through my room, and the kitchen, and where the printer is. I don't think anything was taken."

"What about your computer?" Tessa asked.

"I left that at school. Come in. I'll have to tell my mum."

Noah hated interrupting his mum at work, and told her he'd notify the police, so she didn't need to come home.

"We'd better not touch anything," Noah said. "Let's go outside."

They sat in three old garden chairs to wait. Mia took out her phone to look at the photo she took of the painting. She enlarged the image, and scanned it section by section, looking at the details.

"Why do you think the person was looking where you said?" Tessa asked.

"Well, if it was the shadow guy we saw last night, the kitchen was where we were. I printed stuff off, he might have been looking to see what we were looking at. One sheet didn't print right the first time, so I put that in the recycle box. As for my room, if I kept the stuff we printed, I'd have it there."

"Do you think they will break into my place, or Mia's?"

Noah shrugged.

Mia, still listening to the talk, said, "They won't go near Captain." That was the family's pet German shepherd.

"I put the stuff in an old case I keep under my bed. I can lock it, so my sisters can't get my stuff. I put it in a folder under all the kiddi junk I still have. Besides, we have alarms."

"I will get new locks for Mum," Noah decided.

Mia looked up from her phone. "I think this is one of her earlier works. Looking from that angle, you should be able to see that new tower complex above the trees."

"That was built...when was it?" Tessa thought aloud. She did a quick search on her phone. "1995."

"Did you feel anything from it when you looked at it?" Tessa asked.

"No. And when we used the lights on our phones to look at, nothing came to mind."

"A dead end then?" Tessa asked.

"It is still information," Noah stated.

They spotted two uniformed officers walking around from the front and Noah rose to meet them.

"We'll head off," Tessa called to Noah. "We'll talk later."

Noah waved to show he'd heard, but he was busy talking to the officers.

Chapter 6 - Finding Clues

Noah waited for his mother to get home, pacing about the house, unable to settle to do anything. The police thought it was likely kids breaking in, ones drawn to Mill Haven by the festival. They'd had a lot of calls since it started. He had a different idea, but he hadn't mentioned it. They would think him hysterical if he mentioned the shadow figure at the window, and the shadow figures that had begun to watch him. They would have disregarded everything he said if he told then the only thing he found to be missing was the blurred scan of an old newspaper picture.

When he heard his mother coming in, he hurried to the kitchen. She'd put a takeaway container of the bench, and was looking around.

"I couldn't find anything missing, and whoever it was didn't make a mess," Noah said.

"The housekeeping money?" Mrs Bennett asked.

"Still there." That was money she hid in her wardrobe, in case he needed to get groceries during the week. "Want a cuppa? Kettle won't take long to boil."

"I would love one. Just as soon as I get out of these shoes."

Noah had a cup ready when she came back and she relaxed gratefully into one of the kitchen chairs. "Mr Tarrant has given me some time off tomorrow so I can see about getting the lock fixed."

"I'll help pay for it," Noah offered.

"It shouldn't cost too much," his mother told him, without refusing the offer. "The officer that saw you came to talk to me. Asked me if I had noticed kids hanging around. That sort of thing. They said nothing had been tossed around or damaged. And I remembered you asking about Tom Nicholls, so I asked how he was going. They laughed and said the old guy still rings from Merimbula up to see what's going on. They promised to mention I had asked after him when he rings next."

"Sounds like the guy is lonely," Noah suggested. Though he thought he knew the real reason.

"Checked out the festival. Mia thought she dropped some of

her pencils at the library yesterday, so we went to look for them." Noah wasn't sure why he chose not to mention the investigation into Clara. "We went out to Parson's Folly yesterday. Mia had never seen the place," he did decide to say. "It's been filled in and sort of landscaped. It looks nice now."

"Yes, I heard they were doing that. The council got a grant or something. I never liked you kids going out there. There were always stories of people being injured by the junk there, or they got sick from the poison stuff they used to dump there. I was relieved when they fenced the area off. That wasn't done until some teenagers were hurt really badly there. It really is...was...a dreadful place."

"You want to know what's funny? While it is all grass and wildflowers now, there's still this old rusty car part buried in the centre."

"Maybe they intend it to be a warning to the drivers that hoon around that road bend. More than one person has gone off the road around there."

Noah made a mental note to look into that. He knew of two – Clara's parents, and her.

He changed the subject. "Mr Westbrook wants me to come into work early tomorrow. So I said I'd come straight from school. He wants to talk to me about something. I can get my own tea from the food truck."

"Okay, dear," Mrs Bennett agreed as she finished her tea and got up to fix their tea for that night,

Tessa had finished tea and was helping with the dishes when her eldest brother came in. An idea occurred to her. He might now have his own place, but he still had a lot of stuff in boxes in his old room.

"Gav," she called out. "What year did you start in high school?"

"Later, sis!" He called back, then she heard him talking to her dad.

He came out when she was setting out to finish some work due the next day.

"I'm ten years older than you, can't you work it out?"

"Maths isn't my thing," Tessa reminded him. "Okay, I will rephrase my question. What years do you have copies of the school yearbook for. I've seen back since I've been there, but I volunteered for the yearbook committee this year and wanted to get ideas from older ones."

"You realise that you are following in my footsteps? I did that in year 11 and year 12. If I think back, I think I ended up with spare copies of years books from before I started."

"Wow! Can I look at them too?" He gestured as if he was summoning her, and headed for his old room.

He stood at the door, scanned the boxes and homed in on one in particular. He opened the box and lifted a stack of flat books.

"Treat them like gold, girl. I want them back."

"I will!" Tessa promised, grinning like an idiot. The earliest year books he had, might just have Clara in them. This might save her having to ask tomorrow.

A niggling idea intruded. It would make it less likely someone would find out she was investigating Clara

Mia missed her grandma. Her mother's mother had understood her, believed in her psychometry. She suspected that her grandma had it too, but her generation, would have found it unbelievable, something shameful. Even so, she had learnt a lot from her Gran. Particularly how to stop getting emanations from everything she touched. It occurred to her now that she needed to reinforce those lessons considering the power of the unexpected visions of the past two days. Her Gran had been relieved that she had two staunch friends in Tessa and Noah. She had once said she thought Tessa had the foresight from her Irish ancestors. Mia had to agree with her on that.

However, her gran wasn't around anymore, so the question she wanted to ask, would need to be asked of her mother. Earlier, she had texted Tessa to send her a picture of the odd looking key she had found in Clara's bag.

"Mum, Tessa sent me a picture of a key she saw. It reminds me of something I've seen. Have you seen a key like this?" Mia showed her mother the picture.

"Where did she see it?"

Daisy Chang's face took on a look that Mia secretly called her 'imperfectly inscrutable' expression.

"Possibly at the festival, I guess," Mia lied. She kept watching her mother's face, and didn't get the 'Is that the truth?' look.

"Mum!" Mia regained her mother's attention from wherever else it had gone.

With a sigh, Daisy Chang reached for something around her neck. "Lucy Yang said you would be asking." She handed a gold chain and key to Mia.

"What's this?"

"It's the key for something your grandmother wanted you to have ...when you were older."

"Why did you never tell me?"

Daisy looked at her daughter, as if just seeing she was nearly grown up. "She said, when the time was right, you would ask about it. Wait here."

Mia was used to obeying her parents, but this time, she wanted to see what her mother was doing.

Mia's eyes went wide when she recognised what her mother carried with great reverence. Her Grandmother's writing desk, was lacquered in bright red, with gold scrolls intricately painted around the sides, and a traditional picture lacquered on the sloping top.

"She left that to me?" Mia hardly believed it. She thought it would have gone to her mother.

"My mother thought it would be useful to your painting and calligraphy. It has been in our family for generations."

Her mother placed it reverently on a low table in the lounge room. "I have a box with papers, pens and inks she wanted you to have with it. I think she hoped you would learn to do ink drawings."

"Oh Mum, I have always loved this. It will always remind me of her."

Daisy Chang smiled, and took an envelope from her pocket. "She had this with her will. It's for you."

Mia reached out tentatively, expecting to feel a renewal of her grief when she touched it. Or the pain she knew her Gran was feeling in her last days. Instead, she felt her Gran's vibrant spirit, like she was still there, to see this moment. She closed her fingers on the envelope and let the emotions wash over her.

In her mind she could hear her gran's voice, feel her presence. "You have a very special gift, child. One day, I hope you will use it to help those with no voice of their own. Stay strong. Be vigilant. Remember what I have taught you."

Daisy Chang nodded in satisfaction. To her, Mia's moment of vision, was the reverence expected of one receiving such a gift. "I know you will take great care of it."

Mia lifted the writing desk and carried it to her room where she made a special place for it on her desk. Then, she just stared at it. Everything else fled from her mind.

"Why now, Gran? Why did I get it now?"

There was no answer, but the earlier vision resonated with her. "To help those who have no voice of their own."

It was what she, herself, had said about Clara.

She was due to join a Zoom meeting with Noah and Tessa, but instead, her fingers tingled and reached for the letter opener. She carefully opened her gran's final letter.

The hand writing was shaky, but still showed the elegance of the script she had learnt so long ago.

The first part was her gran expressing regret that she would be unable to see her grow up, and telling her joy at watching the younger Mia, recalling special memories. Then the tone grew more serious, talking about the special gift they shared.

Finally, "I was asked to look over a friend's precious things. The friend sensed wrongs, and wanted to make them right. Instead, I fear, the darkness she saw, finally claimed her. Knowing I could do little to help her quest, she told me she'd hidden precious pieces of herself at the places that spoke to her. Hints of truths, long buried, never spoken of. Records of voices that have been silenced. She left me the key. Now it is yours. Tread carefully, walk wisely, and trust cautiously. Your loving Grandmother, Lilac Yang Chang."

Mia's eyes were streaming as she finished reading. She carefully refolded the letter, and slid it back in the envelope. Only then did she take the key, and insert it in the tiny hole, hidden amongst the ornamental scrolls at the front of the desk.

She expected to see the beautiful paper, elegant pens and the tiny bottles of black, blue, purple and green inks she remembered seeing in there. Instead, there was a palm sized writing journal, a roll of small pages and another odd looking key.

One touch, when moving to pick up the top journal, sent a jolt through Mia.

"No! These are Clara's! How did Gran know her?" Then she recalled the cryptic mention in the letter. "Clara! She was like me!"

The rest of the abrupt jolt unwound.

She saw Clara, or rather heard her and saw her Gran. "These are important. I have to keep them safe for now. I know too much for somebody's peace of mind. I am going to talk to someone, tell them what I know. They have to act. He has to be stopped."

The vision faded, Mia was able to open the first journal. It was a list of her paintings, with a page for each, starting with the one that won her an award, and which hung at the school. She had details of the topic or theme, what was in the scene painted, when the painting was done, and what the weather had been. Pages and pages of such notes.

Mia replaced that one in the desk, and took out the one under it. She opened it at a random page, and saw it was a diary or journal. She almost closed it, in respect for the writers private thoughts and feelings but Clara was missing, likely dead. Clara needed her to read on.

She flicked to the end, more than half of the lined book was blank pages. She flicked back to the last entry.

"He has agreed to see me, and hear me out. If he agrees to investigate, I will bring what I have to show him."

She began to read on, moving backwards, entry by entry. The entries were cryptic, but seemed to start to make some kind of story. Then her phone rang, breaking the trance like state where she felt she almost had the answer.

With a start, she saw the time. She hadn't even set up her computer to join the Zoom meeting, or noticed the SMS with the link.

"Hi Tessa, I'm just setting up now," she said, answering the call. "I've just been ... oh, I'll explain when I join the meeting."

Chapter 7: Clara's Journal

Mia's computer connected, and on her screen she saw Noah's face, and a background of the faded green paint in his room. Tessa's face had a white wall behind, with the corner of one of her athletics posters showing. They would see her with the dragon poster behind her, watching over her.

Noah greeted her first, with his ready grin. It always made her feel lighter. "Thought you'd forgotten. But now we're all here, I'll tell you a few things." He mentioned the outcome of the police visit, how they thought it was kids breaking in. Tessa huffed at that.

"Mum spoke to them later. She remembered me asking her about Tom Nicolls, so she asked how he was going. He's living in Merimbula. We might be able to track him down there."

"And I have Gavin's school yearbooks, plus a few from before he actually started there. Those earliest ones did have Clara in them. I think I might have the names of her closest friends. Rachel Jacobs was one, I think Augustine Garner was another. I took photos of some pages of the book, class photos and class lists. In her year twelve year book, they had an article about her winning that art award. Actually, while that caught my attention, what was on the opposite page did too. It was a mention of two students who'd died. One was riding his bike and was hit by a motor bike, and the other had a severe allergic reaction."

Noah asked, "Do you remember the names of those guys?"

"Ah... let me look." Tessa turned away from the webcam to reach for something. "Bradley Cook and Turner Miles. Know them?"

Noah shook his head. "Make a note of the names. It does seem odd, two dying. Mia, you've been quiet. Did you find out anything about the key?"

"Clara was like me!" was the blurted answer that startled her friends.

"How..." Tessa stopped to try to word the question cautiously.

"My gran knew her." Mia spoke slowly, putting all she had recently learnt into a coherent order. She was still feeling overwhelmed.

"Clara's diary!" Tessa's eyes glowed with excitement, as she leant closer to the webcam.

"There was one that had a list of all the paintings she did – a page for each, with what the picture was, where it was painted, when – the day, date and year, even the weather that day. There were dozens of pages. The other was cryptic, or at least the few I read were." She summarised the contents of those.

"Go back further, pick any page," Noah suggested.

Mia looked down at the book, and flicked an uncounted number of pages. One drew her and she began to read. As her voice was picked up by the microphone, her thoughts revealed a world that felt both familiar and hauntingly distant.

"I feel so alone sometimes. It is as if everyone around me is moving on and I am stuck in place."

Mia glanced at her webcam, the two faces of her friends had expressions blending curiosity and concern.

"This is...really personal."

"Keep going," Noah urged, his hazel eyes intent. "This could help us understand what happened to her."

Mia took a breath and continued, her voice steadying. "I can't shake the feeling that I've lost something precious, something I can't even name. I thought we were close, but maybe it was all a lie." The words hung in the air, heavy with unspoken truths. "A betrayal. I don't know how to confront it."

"No wonder she felt isolated," Tessa murmured, her brow furrowing. "It sounds like she had a fallout with someone important."

Mia nodded, her heart aching for the girl whose life had become a mystery.

"Does she mention who she was talking about?" Tessa asked.

"No. Clara never mentioned names in any of the entries I read."

"Read on a bit," Tessa encouraged.

"Something happened last night," Mia read. "I can't decide what was real and what was not. Did I really see her? The lady in white? Or was she a vision? She spoke of treasure...hidden gems...stolen from them. No, it had to have been a dream or rather a nightmare. I saw my friend, and a shadowy figure dragging her away, as she called back to me. I don't recall her words, my own head was feeling weird, and my eyes were going in and out of focus as if I had taken some drug. All I knew then was that I had to leave...before they came back for me. I must have scrabbled around for my stuff, and got away somehow.

"This morning I woke up, on dirt behind a pile of rubbish. I called dad, and he picked me up. He was angry, but I told him I hadn't taken anything. He demanded to know who I had been seeing. I knew I had to tell him. My friend, if he was that, had to be part of the darkness and never intending to help me like he promised.

"When I looked in my bag, I found a roll of flimsy paper squares. Homemade, thin and fragile. They all looked blank, but they were keys to some hidden treasures. They were calling to me to find them.

"The darkness though, I came too close to it. I am one person, trying to help many. What if I can't? I have sensed the darkness in many places, and many times the ones I called friends went away. I ask why, but people only stare, or turn away. Why?

"If anyone reads this, look at my clues. Maybe you can spot what I cannot and find where the treasures were taken."

"Treasure?" Noah asked, a sparkle igniting in his eyes. "I wonder what she means by that. Whose treasure?"

"Something to do with her friendships, secrets buried in the past," Mia replied, her fingers tracing the words as if they might reveal more than ink on paper.

"Was there anything else with the journals?" Noah asked.

"Just another key."

"What kind?" Noah asked.

Mia took it from the writing desk and held it up. She saw her friends squinting to look at it, then shaking their heads. Noah looked down from the camera and tapping could be heard as he started a search.

"I took a screen shot and I'm doing an image search," Noah explained. "That wasn't much help, but I don't think it's a house key. Mum has to see about a new lock, maybe I can ask what sort of key it is."

He was still thoughtful as Tessa asked, "What does she mean by clues?"

"I haven't had time to read much," Mia pointed out. "I will skip through this to see if anything jumps out at me. But I don't think she wrote them in that journal."

"Don't forget we have school tomorrow," Tessa told her. "It's late already. Let's talk at school or after school before the elective sessions."

"I have to hurry off," Noah told them.

"Oh, yeah," Tessa recalled. "What about we do this again tomorrow. Same time, so we can catch each other up on anything we find."

They sat at a table out in the sun. Around them, students were discussing the festival, laughing and blissfully ignorant of concerns outside of themselves. Noah kept his voice low, as they continued their conversation.

"That's just it, if the clues were so important, why not keep them with the journal?"

"If she wrote that in her private journal, it's like she expected someone might read it," Tessa argued. "But if she thought that, she would want it to be someone she could trust to follow on."

"It was," Mia said quietly.

Noah stared at her. "Yes...it was."

"This is weird," Tessa said. "Like it was predestined that we would go and see that rusty old car."

"Or that's what started it," Noah modified.

"Or it needed someone like me," Mia went on quietly. "Clara knew my gran. Gran knew what I could do. She told mum not to mention the bequest to me. I would ask about it when the time was right. When I wouldn't be alone, like Clara."

"And maybe when people's memories faded," Noah proposed.

"But have they?" Tessa argued, her eyes flicking across the arc of area she could see, checking for shadowy watchers. "It must have been the mention of her name that got people watching us."

The sunlight started to dim, but there were no clouds. She felt the tension in her gut, just thinking about finding Clara. Then the bell rang for the end of break, and the sense of increasing danger fled.

"Our art teacher wasn't teaching here when Clara was still at school. I said I was interested in trying the style of her picture. I showed her the photo I had of the picture hanging at school and asked her what she thought had made it win," Mia told her friends over the Zoom link. "That's when she recalled what she had been told about Clara. She said the picture had an unusual depth of perception, probably because she was such a troubled girl."

"Hey, that doesn't sound right," Tessa blurted. "We all read the letters from the vigil. They describe someone bright and happy."

"I wouldn't say she was troubled either," Noah agreed. "But people can show a different persona outwardly, and still hide troubles."

"I'm just telling you what I was told," Mia shrugged.

"I suppose, if troubled implied depressed," Noah considered, "it might suggest a reason why she vanished. There was that letter from her friend, at the vigil."

"Maybe we need to speak to Rachel or Augustine," Tessa suggested. "I might talk to Cassie first. I'll try tomorrow. Anyway, I showed Mr Joffrey the older year books and the article on Clara. He hadn't heard of her. So I commented on the two obituaries. He didn't think that sort of thing was really appropriate, that it could upset other students. He said it was fortunate that nothing like that had happened since he took over editing the yearbook."

"I guess that's likely," Noah considered, but a vague thought ticked his memory. "Do you remember a kid named Colin something, back in year 7? And rumours went around that he had vanished and his parents wouldn't say anything?"

"Not really," Tessa said. "What's your point?"

"Well the teachers told us he had changed schools, but he didn't go over to either of the other two schools here in Mill Haven, and his parents still live here. So he should have been around during holidays even if not during term time."

"He probably made new friends," Tessa argued.

"It could be nothing, I suppose. Anyway, I spoke to Clarrie. When I got there, he asked me, 'What have you stirred up?'"

"What did he mean?" Mia asked. "We've hardly done anything, so why would he have heard anything?"

"Exactly, he told me, 'no one wants to stir the waters by talking about that girl. No good comes to anyone who gets too close to her.' I told him we were just interested in her art," Noah went on. "He gave me a really odd look, and asked what got me onto that idea. I mentioned the old car in Parson's folly."

"Did he say why it was still there?" Mia asked.

"He sighed and told me it's not worth the idea of doing that car up. It wasn't fixable. I asked if he had looked at it after the accident. He'd gone out, and still said it was fine, and he'd only checked it two weeks before. He said, the poor lad had been drinking. He didn't even mention Clara."

"I still think the police should have had it towed out for a proper check," Tessa countered.

"That was something else he said. They couldn't get a tow vehicle in because the ground was still unstable under the layer of dirt. They would be risking the ground collapsing."

"Could that have happened to Clara?" Mia asked. "No one has found any trace of her."

Tessa felt a prod from her foresight. "Wouldn't they have noticed a hole or something and checked it?"

Noah shrugged. "Lucas arrived then and Clarrie told me to drop it and not ask questions or I would learn, like he did."

"Learn what?" Mia asked.

"I thought I'd better do as he said since Lucas was there. In any case, he got to the reason he wanted us there early. He's sold the repair shop as of that day. He gave us two weeks' pay in lieu of notice, and he had spoken to someone about a job for him and gave him a reference. He told me he'd spoken to the guy at the spare parts place about taking me on, and had a reference for me too. All we did today was clean up around the place."

"Has he been talking about retiring?" Tessa asked.

"No."

"Sounds like he got warned off," Tessa said. "Particularly since he'd heard about what we are doing."

"He might have been," Mia shivered. "We need to keep checking for watchers. I didn't see any after art class, but Dad picked me up."

"Same," Tessa echoed.

"I didn't notice anyone, but I was still taking in the news the shop was closing. I am going to have to get in touch with the spare parts guy, about the job."

"So what can we do now," Mia asked. "I was thinking we could go and look at Clara's house. Check the key that was in her bag."

"Yes, let's do that. We can't stop now. If there is some kind of treasure linked to Clara's disappearance, we need to find the clues she mentioned."

"We can't go inside," Noah told them, hiding his own shiver, and the memory of when the police had picked him up with Cory.

"No, but we could try the key in the lock, and check out the back yard," Tessa insisted. "We might find the clues there."

"I don't know," Noah said, no longer sure they should go anywhere near there. He did know where Clara's family home had been and that it had been empty since Clara disappeared. The shadow watchers would know too.

"We owe it to Clara," Mia interjected, her voice soft but resolute. "She deserves to be remembered, and maybe, we'll find something that will give us answers to what happened to her."

"I know it could lead to something dangerous," Tessa admitted, her protective instincts kicking in. "We don't want to risk our safety. We will need a really good reason to be in that garden, if someone sees us and calls someone."

They shared glances, full of determination and apprehension.

"You're right, Mia," Noah said, looking at her face on the computer. "We can do this together. We've faced challenges before."

They each nodded.

"Tomorrow after school. Let's meet at the café and go for a stroll after that."

It was agreed, and after discussing innocent reasons to end up at Clara's place, they all signed off.

Noah sat back, still determined, but also aware their earlier challenges had had the same potential danger.

Chapter 8: Clara's House

As far as they could tell, no one followed them. They went down a back route through an older section of Mill Haven. When they arrived at the place, one of the homes built on the site of one of the earliest stone and wood houses. It looked a sorry sight. Steeped in memories of death and a life interrupted.

It was at the end, of an overgrown driveway. There might have been a path once, leading to the front door, But it was obscured by tall weeds and flowing shrubs gone wild.

The weatherboard part of the house showed the years of neglect, with its peeling paint and sagging roof. Vines that once grew neatly on an arched trellis, now reached back to the house, through broken windows as if reaching for something lost.

Noah pushed open the creaky iron gate of the driveway, after they had all looked around for watchers. The rusted hinges protested loudly, and resisted movement due to the crowding, untended plant growth and a broken hinge.

"Wow, it's like a jungle," Tessa remarked, her eyes scanning the chaos of a once tended garden gone wild. A hint or rose and lavender reached her nose. "This was probably beautiful once. Now it's just sad."

A tiny meow seemed to echo in the quiet. Mia put her hand in her shoulder bag to comfort the tiny, just weaned kitten she'd found just out of town.

"Clara loved this place," Mia whispered, moving closer to the house. "Her parent's loved it here." Her mind was full of hints of the close family life. She could almost sense their lingering essences.

They followed the driveway down to a garage with a sagging wooden door, then turned into the back yard. It was only partly overgrown thanks to a wide stone patio about the rusty hills hoist clothes line.

"Let's look around," Noah directed.

Tessa headed for the back door, and Mia towards what once had been a herb garden. The kitten in her bag meowed for attention, and she put it down on the ground. It wobbled around on its tiny legs, sniffing at the new place. It meowed plaintively.

"What do you sense here," Mia asked the kitten. It gave no reply, just trotted to a clear patch of dirt to do its business. Then it took off towards where Noah was trying to force his way through to a massive oak tree. "No you don't," she told it, making a grab for it and missing.

"I'll get it," Noah promised, though the tiny creature could go under the thick over growth.

The kitten found the tree and climbed up, just within Noah's reach, but he had to get close to the tree. His foot kicked something metallic as he reached up.

He had just grabbed the squalling kitten when a voice full of authority asked, "What are you kids doing here?"

Noah looked around, recognised both the officers, but needed to get a better grip on the kitten before he answered.

Mia urged, "Bring it here."

Tessa told the officers, "We saw the kitten out front, but it took off. Then we heard it meowing."

Noah ducked down to feel for what he had kicked, and grabbed the square box with his free hand. Then he began to extricate himself. He dropped the box just before he emerged, and also kicked off one shoe.

"There!" he said, giving the kitten to Mia. "If it takes off again, someone else can go after it."

Mia, wide eyed and innocent looking, asked the officers, "Do you know of anyone missing a kitten?"

Their expressions became less severe.

"Out here? It's probably from one of the feral cats," one officer said. "If you are thinking of keeping it, you should get it checked by the vet, and neutered."

The questions changed to, "Where were you headed?"

Noah said blandly, "Just down to the creek. Mia wanted to see some of the old miner's cottages."

"They eyed Mia.

"I wanted to sketch them." Mia gave the kitten to Tessa, and took out her sketch book and opened it to show one of her sketches, and flicked through to the one drawn at Parson's Folly.

"These are good," the officer commented.

The other one recognised Parson's Folly and the angle of the view. His fingers tapped the page. "You really should keep away from there. The ground isn't safe."

"Even after they filled it in?" Tessa asked, innocently.

The officer recited the history of Parson's Folly and were satisfied when both girls shivered realistically.

By unspoken agreement, Noah, Mia and Tessa didn't discuss their visit to Clara's house while they walked home. Instead, they made a fuss of the kitten. The box Noah had picked up was now in Mia's bag.

Had anyone been close enough to hear, it would seem the reason he turned and began walking backwards was to tease the girls about the kitten. He was actually scanning the scene behind them, even as the girls were scanning the front and sides of their route.

They all assumed someone had seen them go into Clara's place. It might have been a neighbour. Two of the places across the street were in a better state of preservation. No one should have seen them from the side blocks next to the property.

If anyone was watching them, they'd had enough chances to see they now had a kitten.

At Mia's house, Noah asked, "Did either of you notice or sense anything?"

"The kitten was scared of something," Mia said.

"I didn't see any one," was Tessa's report. "But that garden was so overgrown, there may have been a way to get in close without being seen. Though, when the officers came, I did get the feeling of being watched, but only until we came out and they went off."

"At least I think the officers bought the kitten story and weren't nosing about, looking to make trouble," Noah gave his opinion. "Let's discuss this later."

Noah waved as he and Tessa headed for her place.

"How's the kitten?" Tessa asked Mia when she joined the Zoom call.

"I'm allowed to keep it," Mia said happily. "Mum loves it."

"Have you looked at the box?" Noah asked.

"I managed to clean it a bit before Mum saw it. It's pretty rusty on the outside. Inside had a kind of felt lining that has been eaten by bugs and is disintegrating. "

"Darn, I hoped it was important," Noah said, deflated.

"It might still be, well, might have been. It was Clara's and she did hide things in it. It looks like whatever she had there was taken and the box discarded. Even so, it still feels important. I am trying to see if the lining will come off, in case something is under it. It's all I can think of."

"Keep at it," Tessa encouraged. "I tried the key in the back door, it didn't fit. I don't know if the front door has a different lock. So far, going there was a bust."

Both girls noticed Noah duck out of view. Through his computer speakers they could faintly hear sirens. Then he was back. "Let's talk later. I want to see where the fire truck is going." His face went off the screen.

Tessa muttered, "He could have told us which way it was going. I hope he knows what he is doing…I have a bad feeling."

Noah's mother was already asleep and he was in two minds about sneaking out, especially since they had not yet had the back door lock fixed. He had rigged a way to stop the door being pushed open, and he could go out the front. He decided to leave a note on the kitchen table. "Heard sirens, sounded close, I am going out to see if I can help."

When he had been younger, slipping out at night had been a habit. He and Cory had learnt to move quietly and avoid notice. The older boy had been like a big brother. Getting arrested had been a wake up. Then, it had been a frightful scare, now, looking back, he guessed they would probably not have charged him anyway.

Cory had apologised for getting him into trouble, and while Noah had been told to stay away from Cory, he had not seen him since then. He wondered briefly if Cory had gone to prison.

Now though, he didn't want to be seen and that skill came back to him. He mentally thanked Cory for teaching him how to go from shadow to shadow, so even the people who had come out onto the street to watch where the fire truck was going, didn't notice him.

The fire glow was noticeable, and he felt a weight in is gut. There was no reason to think it was Clara's house...but it was in that direction. Noah slipped down to the back road and trotted faster. He didn't go too close, just enough to confirm his fear. It had to be Clara's house. He debated going closer, but prudence told him he couldn't help, and so he hurried home.

Once back, he removed the note from the bench and checked that his mother was still asleep, before heading to his room. He took a good look around to check it was just as he had left it, and sent a text message to Tessa and Mia. As he did, he saw he had a message from Mia. At first he didn't understand the picture she'd sent. Then his phone rang.

"There is a map, under that lining," Mia said in an excited whisper. "I'm going to copy it. Okay?"

"Great!" Noah tried to sound enthusiastic. He was still thinking the reason why Clara's house had been torched, was because they had been there. Was someone afraid something might still be there?

Mia hadn't reacted to his message, but as soon as she hung up, Tessa called.

"Is it true?" she demanded.

"I'm pretty sure it is, but I don't understand why. The house has been there, locked up for ten years. If anyone was afraid something was there, they've had all that time to search. And why tonight? When we were just there?"

"Do you think it's a warning?"

That idea made horrible sense. "Could be," Noah had to admit, but to defuse the sudden tension, he asked, "Did Mia tell you what she found?"

"No..."

Noah told her and heard her intake of breath.

"That clever girl! I wonder what else had been in it."

"I don't know. Let's talk—" he broke off, hearing a knocking at his front door. "Got to go."

Noah hurried to answer the knocking, hoping his mother wasn't disturbed. It was too late.

She was up, and had turned on the outside light so she could look through the peephole in the door.

When the door was opened by his mother, seeing the officers gave Noah a real turn.

"What's up?" he asked, as if he had no guilty thoughts.

"Can we come in?"

Noah glanced at his mother, who nodded.

"Sure, come in. How can we help you?" She invited, pulling her dressing gown tighter around her.

"We would like to talk to your on, Mrs Bennet."

"What about?" she demanded, sounding cross because she had been roused from sleep.

"Come out of the cold draught. We can sit in the front room," Noah invited.

His mother sat in her favourite chair, but Noah stood, and confronted the officers.

"You wanted to talk to me? What about?"

"We understand you were at the old Benson house earlier today."

"Oh, the old place – big block, overgrown?"

"Yes."

"I was there. Only went in after the annoying kitten."

"You caught it?"

"Yes, half way up a tree. Mia took it home. Why?"

"Did you notice anything odd there?"

"Not that I noticed. I mean the place was overgrown. I had to bash through some of it to get to the oak tree and the kitten."

"What about the house?"

"We were at the back. We could hear the kitten but not see it. Tessa went to check near the back steps, I was looking in the bushes."

"Did she say if the door was open?"

"No, I think she would have if she thought the darn thing might have gone inside."

"Have you been out again this evening?"

That question gave Noah another jolt.

"Briefly," he decided to admit. "I heard the fire truck and went out to see where it was going. It sounded close, and I went to see if I could help in any way."

"How far did you go?"

"Just until I could see where the glow was. Why? Was the fire at the house we went to?

They didn't say, but they didn't have to. He would have guessed, even if he hadn't already been sure.

He was asked to outline his time that afternoon, and he did. He left out their intent to go to the house, stating they were just out walking, and the fact they hadn't found the kitten right outside the house. Nor did he mention picking up the rusty box.

"We will have a word with your friends," came the decision. It sounded more like a threat.

"At this hour?" Moira Bennet asked sharply. "They've got school tomorrow, as does my son."

"Tomorrow will do," was the placating decision. "It will be to your advantage not to mention our interest."

"I don't want to get them in trouble with their folks. Both Mia and Tessa have a 10pm phone curfew," Noah said emphatically. "Besides, they can't tell you anymore than I have already." He shrugged off the implied threat.

He was relieved when the police car had driven away from the front of the house, but only until his mother asked, "What have you got yourself into?"

"Nothing that I know of," Noah told her truthfully. He briefly mentioned showing Mia the car in Parson's Folly, telling her that is was supposedly Clara's. She'd gone to his school and had a picture of hers on display, and had supposedly vanished.

"Her again!" Moira Bennet shook her head. "Thought we'd heard the last of her."

"What about her?" Noah asked.

"Just talk," she answered. "You hear bits and things at the café. None of it was good."

"I can't see why it matters now. My being at her house was a fluke."

"Forget about her. She's long gone. Get yourself to bed, you have school tomorrow."

Chapter 9: The Map

"It's a map," Mia told her friends. "No names are marked, but I am sure it is a map of Mill Haven. Points are shown as dots. We would need to get a map to compare it to. She was really clever, etching it on the metal and enamelling it. Getting it onto paper may have skewed it. Here, I have a copy for you both."

Mia slipped them both an envelope, then stopped talking as a group of their class mates came close enough to jostle Noah.

"What have you been up to, Bennett? I heard the cops were at your house last night." They didn't wait for an answer, just smirked and rode off laughing.

Mia and Tessa eyed him, he hadn't mentioned the previous night yet.

"Okay, you know about the fire? It was Clara's house, and since we were seen there, and that happened..."

"It's a warning," Tessa said in a low voice.

"I agree. Anyway, the police might talk to you. They didn't want me pre-warning you and I thought I better not. It was way after ten anyway. I didn't get the feeling they really thought I was involved, but I reckon someone saw me go out. They knew I had, so I didn't lie. I told them the truth earlier, except the bit that we planned to go to Clara's place. I didn't mention the box, and implied the kitten was near Clara's when we found it. I owe that cat a saucer of milk for being the perfect cover."

"My father will be angry." Mia seemed to shrink.

"We've done nothing illegal," Tessa told her fiercely. "Someone is causing trouble to scare us off. Do you want to give up?"

"No! I don't. Clara deserves to be vindicated."

"It sounds like what they did to Clara, ruining her friendships and her reputation. Someone must have learnt that she knew things that threatened somebody. We might not have her clues, but if we can identify the places on the map, we can visit them. Who knows what we might uncover."

"We still need to be careful," Tessa warned. "We need to keep a record of what we do, what we find. Each of us. And keep it safe –on our phones, saved online somewhere, multiple places," Mia insisted.

"I don't want you two in danger," Noah's protective instincts caused him to admit.

"We have to do this together," Tessa countered. If it was just you, it would be all too easy to put you out of the way. Like Clara!"

"Yes, it's like you just said. If you read between the lines, everyone that Clara got close to, either died, went away, or turned against her. She had no one," Mia said passionately.

"I have no idea what we will find, "Noah admitted, "but I am coming to believe it won't be nice. We are probably being watched, even when we are doing nothing to bother them. They probably have watchers at places they think might reveal something, like that guy in the woods. Him and that guy near the ponies at the festival. I saw someone with the same type of clothes picking up scattered rubbish along the nature strips outside the school. But, after school tomorrow, we'll figure out the first location and check it out."

The bell went and they headed towards their classes, but they shared a silent agreement, a pact. The thrill of the hunt for clues, carried a whisper of danger looming just out of sight."

The goal was to tell Clara's story, to remove the darkness that shrouded her life, but the stakes had been raised, and they felt they hadn't really started.

The warm breeze ruffled the map they had spread out on the picnic table. Tessa held down her copy if the map from the tin. "This has to be the place," she insisted. Beyond her was Mill Haven Lake, a popular swimming place in warm weather. Families came there on the weekends in summer for picnics.

All three of them looked around, wondering what about the place was important. There was laughing and splashing, but nothing to suggest a source of the darkness they felt.

"Something happened here," Mia said as Tessa folded the map.

Noah rolled up the bought local map, shoved it under his arm and then sat at the table to fiddle with his phone. He typed Mill Haven Lake into his phone's internet browser, and hit search. He scrolled down past all the tourist hype, its origin as a former open pit mine, and the recreational facilities.

"Hey, listen to this."

He had the instant attention of his friends. "It says here, twin girls disappeared around here, 15 years ago. The parents were blamed for not watching them, and they even dragged the lake near the edges, but it gets really deep in the middle. The girls were wearing Disney backpacks and they weren't found either."

Mia wandered closer to the lake, stopping next to a wide, old, oak tree. Tessa watched her as she asked, "What happened to the parents?"

"The mother overdosed 6 months later. The father lost his job just after the girls vanished. His boss claimed he was using drugs, and it was against company policy. They did a follow up, and the guy can only get low paying jobs. His life went to pieces."

Tessa nudged Noah, and pointed at Mia. They both hopped of the picnic table and where she was standing rigidly, touching the tree. She relaxed when she sensed them arrive.

"I know where Clara's clues are," she whispered. "They are in her paintings. She did one here."

Mia pulled her phone out and scrolled through a file of images. "Here! This page of that journal." She read from the image, words Clara had written, describing the very scene around them with extra details.

"A blue and green tartan picnic rug, two Disney backpacks at the foot of the oak tree, the little girls chasing around the parents, clad in orange dresses."

"Did she read about these events, or see them?" Noah wondered aloud.

"Did the paper mention their clothes?" Mia asked.

"Huh!" Noah checked. "No. Does that matter?"

"They were orange," Mia said flatly.

"You saw them," Tessa said.

"Yes, and that same shadow form I saw in the kiosk mural...was watching them.

"Clara's diary didn't mention that," Noah challenged.

"No, but if we find that picture, I bet it will be there."

"What does it mean," Tessa asked.

"IT means that someone out there doesn't want to be found. Someone who is doing things to people, to control them, making then too afraid to challenge him," Noah said. "I bet it starts with making people afraid. Like putting the police onto them even if they are innocent."

"But how can we prove it if we haven't got the pictures?" Tessa asked. "Even then, how can they be proof of anything?"

"It shows a connection," Mia pointed out. "That one person is behind all these things."

"The shadow figure? Is he also the one that has been following us?"

"No." Noah shook his head. "The one behind this is like a spider in his web, when he gets aware of someone interfering, he sends someone out to deal with it. Like the guy in the woods. I bet he had people at the festival for some reason and it was just bad luck we started this then."

"Is there another place we can go to?" Mia asked. "We have to check as many places as we can."

They looked at Mia's transcription of the map, and compared it a map of the local area.

"I think...maybe around near the mini rail. You know, the historical Mill Haven Rail Station."

"Okay, that's just around the lake," Noah agreed.

They had their bikes with them, to give them more time to get around to any other locations they could identify. With their maps and gear stowed in back packs, they rode off along the bike path, seeming like a lot of other day trippers.

When they got to the area, they stopped to look at the fenced off area where the miniature train was chuffing around a circular track, drawing carriages full of young children. The parents were watching from outside the fence.

"I remember this," Tessa recalled. "Particularly the first time I was allowed to go on by myself. I used to have to go with Daniel. They have souvenirs and stuff in the station. They might have a map there of historic sites."

"Okay, let's park the bikes and look around," Noah decided, pointing to a bike rack. They wheeled the bikes over and drew a chain through all three front wheels.

"Let's go inside," Mia urged.

They sidled past the parents waiting to buy tickets for the train to go inside, then edged between those looking at the stands of souvenirs.

Noah nudged the two girls, and nodded at the far wall. Above people's heads, they could see the top of a huge mural. Maps forgotten, they walked between more people to get a clearer view. Mia went to the right most edge, to check for a signature, and nodded back towards her friends. The huge picture of a train at a station had been painted by Clara. The three of them examined the details, and listened to casual talk.

A male voice explained to a couple, "A local artist, did that."

Tessa looked around, saw a youngish man, dressed like a miner from back in the early 1900s. She was about to tell him who the painter was, when she saw Mia shaking her head.

"It's good," she said instead. "Actually, I would have though most artists would have painted the train from the station side."

"Oh, that was done too. It's outside. This side shows what the public usually don't see. That man with the light is looking the train over, before it heads off with a full load of ore."

"How clever. So, outside on the other side of the wall, it shows the other side of the train. I have to see that!"

"I'll show you," the man offered, and Tessa suddenly felt a shiver. She saw Noah and Mia ready to follow, so said, "Okay."

The outside mural had been glassed over to protect it, and there was a low wood log fence to keep people away from it.

"I have got to try doing something like that," Mia exclaimed. "It's brilliant. How long ago was this done?" She sounded exactly like am excited ingénue.

The young man realised he had more company than just Tessa, and moved a step further away from her. "Oh, would have been about ten of fifteen years ago," he said. "This side represents when the railway was opened - the new meeting the old."

Noah managed to get a good shot of it, with his phone camera. He had the man just at one side. Mia leaned over the low wood rail, trying to see more detail. Her eyes went directly to a man, clad in elegant clothes, leading a woman in a long dress of a more modern style. They were arm in arm, and it seemed he was leaning down to listen to her. Other figures in the picture were dressed in a more contemporary style.

Tessa still felt like the man was breathing down her neck, so she called out to Mia. "Do you want another look inside?"

"Yes," Mia said, coming over. "I also want a drink."

Noah suggested, "Why don't you two stand in front of the picture. I'll take a photo."

The strange man quickly moved aside, but he didn't realise it was already too late. Noah had already caught his face. Tessa and Mia came over to look at the shot.

"Send me a copy," Tessa asked him.

Both girls gave the man no more attention.

"We'll have to start getting back," Mia chatted. "But I would like to come back."

Once inside again, the strange man seemed to disappear amongst the visitors. Mia found a seat next to the inside mural, and waited whilst Noah went for drinks.

"That guy was creepy," Tessa said quietly to Mia.

"I think he wanted to get you on your own," Mia told her. That's why we have to stick together. I want a photo of this picture, can you take one of me in front of it?"

"Sure, go over there."

Mia chose her position carefully, so she was next to the lantern wielding man. This picture was also glassed over, but she could touch the glass and did so – right where the light was. She joined the others as Noah returned with the bottles of water.

Wordlessly, they decided to leave and waited until they were riding away from the lake before talking.

"What's with the farmer outfit?" Tessa blurted. "Is it because the mini train is at a historic place?"

"Maybe that's it," Noah considered.

"No, it's creepy. That gut felt intense."

"What he said about the picture," Mia commented. "That was a memorised speech."

"So?" Tessa asked.

"It's not all he was told. The guy with the light? He was told that was the 'reaper', and did you notice, in the picture, that guy was wearing the same type of clothes as the guy who was speaking to you?"

The three bikes slowed to a stop.

"Fits with the historic theme," Noah shrugged. "Though, not the 'reaper' idea."

"Maybe," Mia temporised. "I tried to get an impression off the mural, but the glass interfered. All I got was 'things happen where no one sees'."

"And you got nothing from the other side?" Tessa asked.

"I was too far away," Mia explained. "But did you notice the well-dressed man who was leading the woman away?"

"Yes," Tessa said, staring at Mia.

"The clothes are like those of the man in the picture of the vigil."

"That's even creepier. Do you think Clara was a little bit like me too?"

Mia considered. "I don't think so. I think she picks up on past emotions. Can we find out if someone went missing from here?"

Noah smacked his forehead. "I'll look at home. We should have thought of that, especially after the lake scene."

"Was that the original location of the station master's house?" Mia asked.

"No, it wasn't," Tessa told her. "I remember hearing they had dismantled it and did it back up there. I think it used to be closer to one of the mines, not sure where, exactly."

"Maybe near the poppet head – the one on the tourist brochures for the history trail," Noah said. "Maybe we need to look there too."

Mia considered. "Yes, I didn't get any feeling of 'bad' at the mini train place."

"It's too far to get to today," Noah calculated. "We will have to plan it for a weekend. We have other places, that are closer, to check still."

"That's okay," Mia decided. "Let me check about those murals back there, in her book. I hadn't read about them."

"Not all her pictures need to be clues," Noah suggested.

"That might be true, but we need to check out as many as we can, even if we don't find a correlation with old news reports. We shouldn't discount any of them."

"I agree," Tessa sided with Mia. "People in town don't want to talk about back then. Like you said about Colin. He vanished, the parents wouldn't talk. Those twin girls the same. It's like they are too afraid to talk, and it's likely even the police don't know of some things."

"Are you implying someone is taking what people most treasure?" Noah's voice was hoarse, just thing of what that might mean. The potential implications, not fully understood, sent fear through all of them. "I think that is what Clara realised."

"Do you think all those who vanished, are...dead?" Tessa asked in a whisper. "Do you think Clara is dead?"

"I don't know any more than you, but no one has seen or heard of her since she vanished."

It didn't feel good.

"Let's get home," Tessa urged. "May try to connect the descriptions of the other paintings to events, without looking for them."

"It might not be enough," Mia said. "But we can try that. We can't stop now."

Chapter 10: Warnings

The next Zoom meeting was mostly a failure. Mia found her computer was going slow and kept dropping out. Finally Noah gave up.

"Let's meet tomorrow, okay? Mia, do you have a virus checker on your computer?"

"Yes."

"Then run it," Noah advised. "Don't try going online until you do."

"I'll log off and do it now." Mia's face vanished from his screen.

"I should do that too," Tessa decided.

"I'll be doing it too," Noah said soberly. "Plus I am going to get a VPN, so if I do more searching, no one should know that I am. See you tomorrow."

Noah ventured out of his room to get a drink from the kitchen. His mother had already heard about his day, but she came into the kitchen just after him, and he sensed something was worrying her.

"What's up?" he asked her.

"I'm just being an old woman," Moira Bennet claimed. "You are almost grown up. I will have to get used to you doing your own thing."

"I'm being careful, mum," Noah told her.

"I know, but like I said, I'm your mother – I just can't help it."

"What brought this on?" Noah asked her.

"Didn't you hear? About the fire?"

"The one the other night?"

"No. At the place where you worked."

"What happened?"

"Oh, it's just that there was an accident. I heard Clarrie got caught under some equipment and a fire started somehow."

Noah felt the blood rush from his face. "Is...is he okay?"

"They took him to the hospital, that's all I know."

"I'll check in the paper tomorrow," Noah said, thinking aloud.

"I am just so grateful you are not working there anymore."

Suddenly, Tessa's idea didn't seem so far-fetched. Was this

another instance of Clarrie being scared off? Was it another attempt to scare him off?

At school the next day, several of his classmates mentioned the fire, but had no new information about Clarrie. He was still worrying about that when Tessa and Mia found him.

Mia was looking mutinous and Tessa determined.

"What's up?"

"She argued with her father," Tessa said, when Mia couldn't find words.

Took a step back. That was serious. Mia was the most respectful and obedient person in the whole school. She respected her parents and their culture.

"Dad told me I had to stop seeing you."

"Because I am some kind of delinquent, thief or something?" Noah guessed. Mia nodded stiffly.

"So..." Noah prompted.

"I told him straight out that whoever had told him the things about you, was lying. I said you were my best friend, along with Tessa, since we came here, and if I had even suspected something like that I would never have disrespected my parents so badly as to keep seeing you."

"Tell him the rest," Tessa urged her.

Mia gave a weird laugh. "At that point, Aunt Lucy told him that of all the boys at school, you were the only one who would never disrespect me."

"Of course I wouldn't," Noah protested.

"I know that! That's what I told Dad. So he just said, if I ever felt differently, to come and tell him. I said I would."

"That better include anyone else if they make you uncomfortable," Noah stressed.

"And in the same vein," Tessa said, smirking faintly. "Someone hinted to my mother that you and I had slipped off to be more than friends."

Noah saw the pattern. "And...?"

"I told her that whoever told her that had a filthy mind. That she could take me to a doctor if she needed proof I was still a virgin. I asked her it was that told her that, and it sounded like one of those pursed lip women that we have seen about the place."

"Do you realise," Noah began, choosing his words, "that someone wants to discredit us and scare us away from investigating Clara's disappearance."

"Or split us up," Tessa proposed, but was still determined not to let that happen.

"Yeah, that," Noah agreed, thinking of the man at the mini train place. "Warn us off is right." He told them about Clarrie and they all fell silent.

"I'm not giving up!" Mia stated.

"Nor am I," Tessa backed her up.

"I'm with you," Noah agreed. "If they are going to these lengths to deter us, they have something huge to hide. It is frustrating that we don't have proof of anything to take to the police, let alone a clue to who is behind it. All we have is a string of coincidences that could be taken as Clara reading about things."

"All the more reason to be her voice," Mia insisted.

"To figure out what she knew," Tessa added.

"And figure out what she missed seeing – or saw –too late," Noah finished. "Do you have your computers at school?"

"Uh, yes," Tessa confirmed, reacting to the unexpected change of subject.

Noah told them what he intended to do, so when they next went searching on line, no one would trace it back to them. "I've bought 3 licences for a VPN. I have the link so you can download it to use. I'll meet you in the library during lunch, okay."

Tessa had athletics practice after school, so only Noah and Mia walked to where the interstate busses pulled in. They looked around, trying to find the angle Clara had used in her picture.

"She couldn't have sat here to paint," Mia decided. "It's too busy. She might have sketched it first."

"Your special touch likely won't help here," Noah predicted.

"No, too many people have been here." Mia was thoughtful as they headed back into town.

"I thought to go and look at the repair shop." Noah didn't sound like he really wanted to. Not since he'd heard of Clarrie being the victim in the fire. He couldn't help but think it was his fault because he had asked about Clara's car.

They stopped across the road. Noah stared at the gutted building, his guts in a tight knot. Clarrie had been good to him, getting him interested in mechanics and cars. First paying him to help clean around the place, and gradually teaching him to do more.

"It could have been us in there," a voice Noah recognised spoke from behind him.

Noah turned to see Lucas Evans, whose face showed no expression. "All because of that bitch..."

"Who do you mean?" Noah asked. Mia watched as Lucas decide if he would answer.

"Ten years on and Clara is still causing trouble for people."

"That seems incredible," Mia told him, trying to be tactful.

"Oh, no," Lucas claimed, looking at Noah. "Did you go into Clarrie's office after we started moving his stuff out?"

"No," Noah admitted.

"He had a picture in there. One of hers. It showed the front of the shop, and the front of the bile store that used to be next door."

"How would that cause problems?" Mia asked.

"Because they want everyone to forget she ever existed."

"Who are they?" Noah asked. Lucas shrugged. "I don't know, but try to talk to anyone over thirty about her and they all clam up."

"How can they?" Mia asked. "There are paintings of hers at school, at the park and the mini train."

"Even that is too many," Lucas retorted. "You're too young to have known her, but she was like poison ivy. Anyone who got too close to her suffered, died, vanished or went away."

Neither Noah nor Mia wanted to mention his brother.

"So if she is to blame, what did she do to them?" Mia argued.

Again Lucas shrugged. He didn't want to answer with details. He spat on the ground, gave the blackened building one last look, and stalked off.

Noah began walking again. Mia scanned her phone screen, walking without watching where she went, trusting Noah to stop her walking into something.

"Here! I found the description." Mia read it out. "Bike shop, repair shop, mangled push bike, damaged motor bike. Late September, overcast. Little cross and flowers."

"Bradley Cook!" Noah blurted.

"Wasn't that an accident?" Mia asked.

"Was it? I will check the local paper to see if the accident was mentioned. Where do you want to go now?"

"There's a picture framing place in the street near the café. I was wondering if Clara went there."

"Are you going to ask right out? Ten years is a long time. And we'd have to be sure no one was listening."

"I will ask about something but out in enough keywords to see if I get a reaction. I was thinking of getting a drawing I did of my gran framed as a present to Mum."

"Well, okay. But then we should head home."

They had to wait for several couples to leave the shop before Mia approached the man at the register. Noah had to admire her deft questioning, and her knowledge of what she was pretending to want. He listened as she discussed colour, frame style, what it was for and cost.

The owner popped out the question. "Is this something for a school art competition?"

"I don't know if I am good enough," Mia said modestly. "Someone from our school won something. It's framed and put up near the office."

Noah noted the deft glance around, and the man's wife going to turn the sign on the door to 'closed'.

"I'll write you out a quote," he said. "Just come through to the office, I have some colour samples there, and style pieces."

Mia glanced at Noah, and gave him a nod. He wasn't sure exactly what she was telling him, but he guessed she thought it was okay. He followed, and began to wonder when the man said, "Wait here, I will get what I wanted to show you."

He came back with an armful of coloured frame pieces resting on a paper covered rectangular shaped parcel.

"Your mention of the school reminded me of something," the man said. He put the pile down and extracted the parcel and carefully cut the sealing tape. "I had this frame sitting around. It was made to order, and paid for but not picked up. I thought it might suit the portrait you mentioned. If you think it will suit, I can give it to you at half price."

Mia's eyes went wide when she saw the picture of the old miner's shack. One quick glance at the bottom corner, confirmed her guess as to the painter. Noah nudged her when he caught sight of the woman approaching.

"It's not a bad colour," Mia said clearly. "I like the style and the size should work, but I was picturing a rich reddish blue shade."

"Ah, excuse me," the man said quickly.

Noah edged to the door and heard the woman say, "...here to talk to you."

He hurried back to Mia. "Cover over the picture and look like you are comparing other colours."

As Mia picked up some of the frame pieces, Noah took a quick photo of the picture.

The man returned. "Well, what do you think?" He sounded over hearty, not like he had before.

"I think I will stick to the darker red," Mia said clearly. "Will you need to order it in?"'

"I will check through my stock. It's not a popular shade. If I don't have anything, I can order it in."

"I'm not quite ready to frame yet, but if you could check your stock, and do me a quote. I can see if I have enough saved up to do it."

"Right, let me sort out a cost for you."

Noah idled near the office door as the man jotted things on a pad, and entered them in a spreadsheet. After spotting the woman talking to the owner's wife, he moved closer to the desk.

"Mr Wells, if I were you, I would take that picture out of the frame and hide it really well."

Wells glanced up, startled. "How did...were you listening?"

"No, but trust me on this," Noah stressed. "I just found out that Clarrie Westbrook had a picture hidden in his office."

Wells face lost colour. He nodded tersely and sent a document to the printer.

He gave it to them and said, "There you are, it's good for three months."

Noah and Mia allowed themselves to be led to the door. Noah caught sight of a figure outside, watching in through the window, but showed no sign. Mia must have sensed his concern, so as they stepped outside, she was looking over the quote and said, "It's more than I hoped. I might have to go with a simpler frame."

The woman Noah had seen was not acting like she wanted to go in, so he paused outside the door to say, "You could ask your dad to help. Offer to pay half."

The woman approached, harrumphed hinting he was being rude. Noah quickly moved and apologised. He hoped he had given Wells enough time to take his hint.

Noah nudged Mia to the nearest corner and used the need to check for cars as a reason to look around for possible followers. He didn't pay attention to the approaching cyclist, never expecting him to deliberately swerve at them. They were just stepping of the kerb when Noah felt the shove. He was off balance and fell into Mia, knocking her over as well. She yelled, feeling her shoulder bag being tugged. Noah rolled off her and lunged after the bike rider, catching him before he got his bike back up to speed. The guy laughed, emptied the bag and tossed it. He had the quote in his hand, but after glancing at it, he released it to the brisk breeze, and shook Noah off.

Rather than try to run after him, Noah knelt down to help Mia collect her things.

"I'm sorry," he told her.

"Not your fault!" she practically spat out the words. "At least he didn't break any of my pencils, and my sketchbook didn't fall out into the gutter."

That she was just on the road and defiantly picking up other miscellaneous girl stuff, drew the attention of a patrolling police officer.

"What happened here?"

Noah recognised the officer, from after their visit to Clara's house. He explained what happened, since Mia's lips were firmly clamped shut. He told them it was deliberate.

"It could have been accidental," one of the officers suggested. "And the bag got caught on something."

'NO!" the usually quiet Mia, exploded. "He grabbed my bag, tipped everything out and rode off laughing." She was holding back tears, and the officers saw it.

"Can you describe the rider?"

Mia considered. "I can do one better."

She took out her smaller sketch book and a black pencil and began to draw. While the two officers watched the face emerge, with a look of amazement, Noah trotted over to where the quote had been caught by a bike rack. He handled it carefully as he returned. Mia finished her quick sketch and handed it over. The officer showed it to Noah for confirmation.

"Yes, that's just like him." Then he added details of the clothes the rider wore and the bike. "And he handled this."

"I have a display pocket," Mia offered, her tone calmer.

"We'll take this with us, if that is all right? Do you want to make an official report?"

"My dad will probably insist, but he will want to come with me," Mia said directly. "And I need to put antiseptic on some scrapes."

"When you are able then, come down to the station, Miss...?"

"Mia Chang," Mia supplied. "My father is Roxton Chang."

Noah guessed the name meant nothing to them. They could look him up and find he was a respected scholar, but they'd not know the power he held in the local Chinese community. He wasn't even sure Mia knew that.

Mia was limping slightly when they got underway, and after a while, Noah realised she was crying silently. He had the strongest urge to wrap an arm around her, but only dared to reach out and take her hand. Mia sniffed loudly, and used her free arm to rub her face with her sleeve.

"I'm sorry. I am just so angry I don't know what else to do."

"No apology needed," Noah told her. "I'm so angry I want to

kick one particular living creature."

"Do you think they will find the rider?"

"Truthfully? No. He'll vanish like all the other shadows we've seen. And if whoever sent him after us realises there is a picture of his face, he will stay vanished and someone else will have to get sore feet following us around."

"He was following us," Mia confirmed. "He was told to find out what was on the paper that guy gave us. I think he confirmed it was just a quote."

"Let's hope so, or we will be reading about another fire."

"Do you think they know about the picture?" Mia's concern now was for the gallery owners now.

"I don't know. Let's hope he had time to do what I said."

"Should we have warned the police?"

"I doubt it would make any difference. All they could do is send out more patrols to drive by. Anyone determined to do mischief could easily avoid them. That's if they even believed us. We'd have to go into what we are trying to do. What we have so far isn't proof. And if was talk now, word could get to the wrong ears."

"They can't make us stop!"

"I really can't think why they think us dangerous."

"Because we are. Have you got an address for that old policeman yet?"

"Let's talk about this tonight. I do think we need to get him on board"

"I'll go through that list of drawings again. I don't recall seeing one that fits that picture. All I felt from it was 'secrets' but that might have been because it was kept hidden for so long."

While Noah was relieved that Mia had recovered her equilibrium, he realised the attack was an escalation in a campaign to make then stop looking for Clara. And she was right, they did need to get someone to believe in what they were finding, before the darkness that got Clara smothered them too.

Chapter 11: Getting Too Close

Mia told her friends about going to the police station to give an official report, ending with, "They know they can't ignore my Dad, now."

Noah didn't ask how, preferring to discuss what they should do next.

"Mum hasn't heard back from Tom Nicholls," he said. "But I have an address, which I think is him, and a number. I will try calling it tomorrow, it's too late to do it tonight. I think, if we can tie a few more of her pictures to events, it should make the police look into it. Surely, even if people today won't talk, the police must have reports from back then."

"I'd like to think that," Tessa told him. "But whoever is behind this wields a lot of power. Police didn't help Clara, that's why someone... us...has to. And I agree that Tom Nicholls sounds like the person we need. He knew Clara, and promised to look after her."

"Then why hasn't he done anything all this time?" Mia demanded.

"We don't know he hasn't," Noah pointed out. "If he is meeting brick walls trying to get people to talk, how much can he do?"

"He went away. Interstate!" Mia argued. They couldn't argue that. "So, yes, sound him out."

"Do we have anywhere else we know she did a picture?" Tessa asked. "I'm not stopping."

"Actually," Noah decide to introduce an idea. "I was wondering if that picture Mia and I saw today – a miner's shack – is anywhere near the old poppet head I told you about."

"We are going to look at that place anyway," Tessa reminded him.

"Yes, but I was thinking, we do nothing we wouldn't normally do for the rest of this week, to lull suspicions. Like we have taken the warning. Then go out really early on Saturday."

"I don't want to stop doing everything," Mia told him. "I feel we are so close to the answer."

Tessa's face took on a worried expression. "What if we are? We don't know the answers yet, but those people we keep seeing, are getting more obvious. They do know what they are hiding."

"That just means, we need to stick together," Noah insisted. "Three of us together is more of a problem for them than one woman. Clara must have figured out things, but left it too late to act."

"Then we cover all the bases," Tessa decided. "When we go out on Saturday, we leave a note or tell someone where we are going and when we expect to be back."

"And we make sure our phones are fully charged," Noah added. "We need to out think the shadows. Maybe if we act like silly teenagers, they will lower their alertness and we can trick them."

"I wouldn't count on that," Tessa warned.

"We won't," Mia promised. "And I will be telling myself and any deity that can hear us, that we are doing it for Clara."

"I don't know what they think we can find out," Tessa mused. "Except at the library, we haven't been obviously questioning people. We have only been going to local places and looking for Clara's pictures."

They all wanted to believe that, but each of them could see the faces of the others on their computer screen, and knew that was no protection.

Still united in their determination to reveal what Clara had discovered, the reason the town's folk wouldn't talk of her and many other things, and even now, ten years on, were afraid – they were not going to give up. Of one thing, they were all sure, what they had found so far was only the tip of the real truth.

Each hid their fear, and reiterated their determination to be Clara's voice.

Early Saturday morning, Noah left to ride to Tessa's place to meet her, then they to go meet Mia. They had prepared as soon as they could. Over the past few days, using Google maps, and local grid maps, they thought they had the rest of Clara's map points identified by GPS location if not by name or description.

Since the old poppet head was their main destination, they chose a route back that went past four other dot locations from Clara's map. They also had a good idea of where the old station master's house had once stood.

Apart from wanting to keep any shadows from seeing them leave, they wanted to do as much as possible before the day's temperature became too hot. They each told their parents where they were going with as much detail as possible.

Mia's father had nearly ordered her to stay home. She told him how she wanted to learn the history of where they now lived. Since he was a scholar and had a deep reverence for his ancestors and the past, he had allowed her to go.

The poppet head. The station master's house and the old mine siding were shown in old photographs of the early days of Mill Haven. Brochures on the history trail, showed them all, but the actual trail no longer went near them. The former had been repositioned, as they knew, but the other points remained at their original location.

The history trail started at the lake and was clearly signposted, and started off as a sealed path. After two kilometres, then became a maintained, unsealed surface. Bikes were allowed, as long as the riders respected pedestrian traffic. Tessa was navigating.

"Here! The old part of the trail goes off here."

They dismounted and wheeled their bikes past the end of a log barrier erected to block the trail. There was a sign stating, "Track closed" and another with a graphic indicating it had washed away or collapsed.

"I wonder what happened," Noah wondered aloud.

"Can't have been all that long ago," Tessa mused.

"How long ago did the move the station master's house?" Mia asked.

"It's been at the rail place since before I was five or six," Tessa said, after giving it some thought. "So, ten years, about."

"Has to be longer, since Clara painted the mural there," Mia corrected. "Though it might have been one of her later ones."

"Let's head up. This first part looks okay," Noah decided.

After about half a kilometre they had to stop. A second log fence stopped them. This one warned, "Washout".

"How far away are we from the first point?" Noah asked Tessa.

"It can't be far, Tessa said after considering the GPS on her phone. "Maybe two hundred metres a\still to go."

"We can leave our bikes here, since we will be returning this way."

As they went ahead on foot, they watched the track ahead for signs of the washout, and for what Clara had considered so important.

"Stop! It should be around here."

Mia looked around and asked, "Are you sure?"

"Maybe it's a bit off," Tessa suggested. "We can look anyway then move on slowly."

Each in their own way tried to decide where they would hide something. Noah checked the side where the ground sloped down. The track had begun to turn in a bend, and he could see a little ahead where there had been an earth slippage. He took out a mini pair of binoculars to study the area. The slippage hadn't been recent for some grasses and saplings were already growing in it. However, in that area, the sun could get through, and lower down, something long and white was starkly visible. He switched his binoculars for his phone and tried to see the spot more clearly. It didn't help, he took a picture at the highest resolution and kept the date and position options on.

Then he heard Tessa exclaim, "I've found something."

She was further ahead on the path, but both Noah and Mia headed to when she was crouched down.

"What is it?" Noah asked, as Mia went to kneel where Tessa was holding back a branch of a bush.

"Looks like a cairn," Noah thought aloud. "Those rocks aren't from around here, they are too smooth."

Mia reached in to touch the cairn. It was small, no more than ten centimetre high and twice that wide. For a long moment she was silent. "There is something here. Something sad."

"Let me get a photo," Noah told them.

Mia began to move the neatly piled rocks, which had over time gathered dirt in the spaces. When she had reached the level of the ground, she saw something like a square plastic lunch box.

"Don't touch it," Noah warned her, before taking another photo. "Let me try to lever it out with a stick."

"It's not likely to blow up, is it?" Tessa joked, as eager as the others to know what was in it.

"It might have fingerprints. Maybe Clara's."

While Mia stopped it from falling back into the place it had been, Noah dived into his bag for his lunch, and transferred one of his sandwiches into the other bag. The now empty plastic bag, was inverted so Mia could use it to pick up the plastic box and give it to him. She then put the stones back neatly before standing up.

"Clara put it there. She found something here."

"Open it!" Tessa urged.

Noah used the plastic to remove the lid. Inside was a piece of folded paper, still looking clean and white. Trying not to touch it with his fingers, he used a twig to open it up while having it on his pack, and another to hold it while opening it further.

"Who is it?" Tessa asked, seeing a sketch of a girl, or young woman's face.

Noah took a photo. "We can figure that out later. I am going to send the photos I took here to each of you, and to an email address I made up a few days ago for use on my computer. Fold that back up and one of you put it in your pack."

The bright sun had lost some of its intensity. "Someone died around here," Mia said quietly.

"This area is on the other side of the hill from Parson's folly," Tessa pointed out, suddenly shivering.

Noah decided not to mention the white thing he had seen that might be a bone.

"Should we keep going?" Tessa asked.

"Yes!" Mia insisted before Noah had a chance to say anything. "That miner's shack might be up here. Maybe that's how Clara found the place where the cairn is."

"Why would she have come this way? It's a long hike from town."

"Did she mention that sketch?" Tessa asked.

"I will look later," Mia said. "Let's keep going."

The land slip seemed to block their way, but Noah, using his mini binoculars, saw where someone had created a narrow compacted path around the top of it. They had to go in single file until reaching the continuation of the wider trail.

"How far to the next spot," Noah asked.

"Maybe a kilometre," Tessa estimated.

The next place was obvious, a wide, old concrete area sat next to the remains of a railway. The stones and decaying bearers remained but the rails had been taken away.

"This must have been where a station used to be," Noah guessed.

Tessa checked the tourist map. "I would say so. The question is, what if anything is here?"

Mia wandered around the concrete then moved onto the old rail bed.

"It might just be a way marker," Tessa guessed. She noticed that Mia didn't seem to be reacting to anything. She raised her brows in a silent question when Mia returned.

"Nothing."

"We'll keep going then," Noah directed.

As the track curved around again, they entered an area thick with trees. Out of the direct sunlight, the air seemed colder and the noises of birds and cicadas was muted. Only a narrow strip of light filtered down from a narrow gap above.

"I think we must have got off the main track," Noah voiced his concern. "I can believe new trees encroaching the track since it was closed, but these trees are too big to be recent growth."

Tessa looked around. "I didn't see any other tracks leaving the station site."

"There was that pile of logs on the other side of the clearing," Mia recalled. "Maybe it was there."

"Should we back track?" Tessa asked the others.

Noah checked the GPS app on his phone. He'd put in the points they aimed for and the app tracked their route. "We could keep going, we are still heading in the right general direction." He glanced at each of the girls.

"Fine," they both decided.

They were all having second thought by the time they finally emerged near the old mine. Noah took a photo, but they wouldn't be going close. The poppet head was fenced around with a high cyclone wire fence. Signs warned against entering.

Beyond the fenced off area was a barn like shed and the abandoned ruin of a shack. Noah directed attention to it as a cloud obscured the sun. He headed that way and took a photo.

"Do you think this is the shack?" Tessa asked Mia.

"No, the one I saw was a different design. This has a door at the end, not on the side."

"Getting anything else?" Noah asked her.

"Nothing specific. I am glad to move away from the min head. It probably had its share of accidents. What I was getting felt old."

A strong gust of wind found its way to where they stood. Noah saw that more clouds had formed overhead. He decided to check the weather radar on his phone.

"We should head back. They've issued a storm warning, and there is heavy rain coming over."

Mia wanted to insist on going on, but she couldn't argue with Noah when he reminded them about the washout section of the track back.

"We'll have a quick look around and get going," Tessa suggested.

Noah nodded, chewing on his lip as he glanced up at the thickening clouds. They loomed overhead, dark and ominous, threatening rain. "We have to find a way to piece it together. Clara wouldn't have left us all these clues if she didn't want us to know something."

Just then, a rustle in the underbrush made them all freeze.

Chapter 12 - Friend and Foe

Mia's heart raced, her instincts kicking in as she turned her head slowly toward the sound. There, partially hidden by the shadows, a figure emerged, stepping into the fading light. He was rugged, with unkempt hair and a face that bore the marks of hardship. His cloths suggested he was a forestry ranger, but the tension in the air thickened. Noah instinctively took a step forward, a protective urge surging through him.

"Who are you?" Noah called out, his voice steadier than he felt.

The figure paused, eyes narrowing as he studied them. "I patrol this area. I saw your bikes. It's not safe up here. You need to leave."

When they didn't react, he went on, "You're poking around in things that don't concern you." His voice was low, his tone one of dire warning. "You should leave any memory of Clara alone."

Mia's breath caught in her throat. "You knew Clara?" The name hanging in the air between them like a fragile thread.

The man stepped closer, his stance defensive. "She and I were friends. More than friends." His words were heavy with a mixture of pain and anger. "You think you can just come here and dig up the past? The town has forgotten her, but I haven't. I won't let you disrespect her like this. Dredging up all the old antipathy. Renewing old pain."

Noah took a deep breath, feeling a swell of determination. "We're not trying to disrespect anyone. We're trying to understand what happened to her."

The man's eyes flickered with something—hurt, perhaps, or maybe just a flicker of hope. "You think you can understand? You don't know anything about her struggles, about how this town turned its back on her."

Tessa stepped forward, her voice firm but gentle. "Then help us understand. If you really cared about her, tell us what you know."

There was a moment of silence, the air thick with unspoken words. The man looked at each of them, gauging their sincerity. Finally, he sighed, the tension in his shoulders easing just slightly, as if he had made a hard decision. "I'll tell you, but you need to know—some truths are dangerous."

Noah exchanged a quick glance with Mia and Tessa, and they nodded, a silent agreement forged among them. They were all in this together, and Clara deserved to be remembered.

"Come over to the old feed shed," he suggested. "The storm is going to be a bad one."

They settled on low stacks of cut wood, a cold breeze coming in the door grounding them as the first heavy drops clanged on the iron roof. Ned—he finally introduced himself—began to recount memories, his voice low and filled with emotion.

"I knew how the town had to be. Somewhere we keep to ourselves, and reject outsiders. Clara was different, you know? She had dreams that no one else understood. She wanted to be an artist, to paint the stories of our town and share them with the world, with outsiders. But here, in Mill Haven, everyone expected you to fall in line, to fit a mould.

"I had to persuade her to change, to conform. To keep her safe, for me."

Mia's heart ached with recognition. She felt a kindred spirit in Clara's struggles, her own artistic aspirations often met with doubt and disapproval. "What happened then?" she asked softly, her voice barely above a whisper.

Ned clenched his fists, his knuckles white against the brown of his uniform. "The last time I saw her, we had a fight. She wanted to leave. She was tired of the whispers, the judgmental eyes. I told her she was being foolish, that no good would come from leaving. I just wanted her to stay, but she walked off on me, told me she never wanted to see me again, that I was a spineless coward like the rest of the town. That was the last time I saw her." His voice cracked, revealing the raw wound of regret.

Noah sensed the weight of Ned's words, the burden of loss and guilt that hung in the air. "Do you think she left town? Or do you think something happened to her?"

Ned shook his head, his expression darkening. "I don't know. If I had been stronger, I would have gone with her. I realised too late she had the right of it. There were people in town who would do anything to keep the truth buried. They didn't want Clara stirring things up, revealing their deep guilty secrets. Clara was a threat to their peaceful life. She wasn't just a girl with dreams; she was a threat to the status quo. I couldn't convince her to let things be. And if you dig too deep, you might find yourself facing the same fate."

Mia reached out a hand, sharing his emotional pain. "They punished you," she said, quietly. Ned nodded.

"I nearly died. Spent 12 months in hospital and rehab. When I was able to return, she was gone and no one would talk of her."

Just as the gravity of Ned's revelation settled around them, a loud crash echoed from out in the clearing, sending a jolt of adrenaline through the group. Ned jumped to his feet, his protective instincts kicking in.

"Hide behind the hay and logs," he warned in a low voice. "Stay quiet," he warned, scanning the shadows that seemed to shift and whirl, as if alive. He strode out of the shed as a loud, derisive voice called out, "Where are you Neddy boy, you craven coward?"

"Here!" Ned announced, when he walked out of the shed.

"Found the brats yet? Or did you throw them down the old mine?"

"No, I've checked here. For all I know they slipped down the old washaway. If they were dumb enough to ignore the warnings, the damn scavengers can have them. I was about to head on to the cabin, or did you check there on the way up?"

The rain that had eased, came down even heavier with a strong gust of wind. If the other speaker replied they didn't hear him. Then the gust passed.

"Go move the bikes," the derisive voice ordered. "If the brats are missed, we don't want the bikes being found around here."

"And what will you be doing?" Ned challenged. "Going back to your snug house?"

"I wouldn't be out if you hadn't fallen down on the job, again. Go move the bikes, There will be a van on the track waiting and be careful you don't become scavenger food yourself."

"Go home and be damned," Ned said.

"Watch yourself, Ned. Respect those who look after you. Come to the cabin when you're done. The leader wants a word with you."

Ned stamped back into the shed, making noises to suggest he

was getting things to take with him. He said nothing to the three hidden youngsters.

"What's with the rope?"

"You want the job done! If water is coming down over the bypass, I might need it to get around."

"Big Hero! Well, hurry off."

The voices stopped, Noah reached a hand to each of Tessa and Mia, to reaffirm they were not alone.

Another gust of wind sent rain right through the open door, into the shed. Lightning lit up the outside for a moment, and they saw a silhouette in the doorway. They all curled into a smaller space.

Hardly daring to breathe, they listened for the slightest sound to suggest the man was coming further inside.

The man, thinking he was alone, started talking again. Snippets carried to unseen ears.

"No, if they came to the mine, they must have gone back down and that fool Ned missed them. I reckon the bikes will be gone when he gets there." A pause, then, "In this? They'll head home. If the rain stops tonight, and they know about the damned wench's cabin, they be back looking for it tomorrow." Another pause. "Of course. They are kids! It won't be hard to get then to tell us what they know."

The speaker must have ended the call, because when he spoke again, his words were loud and definitely not respectful. He sounded as if he was too important to have to be out in a downpour, and cursing the fact his car was a fair walk away. The tirade continued, until the rain eased to drops, then it stopped and the overwhelming sense of menace retreated.

Tessa spoke in a very quiet whisper. "We need to get out of here."

Mia said, "Which way can we go, after that...vile man, or back the way we came?"

"Mia, did you pick up anything from Ned? Do you think he was tricking us?"

"No. His pain was real."

"But he sounded like he was looking for us, and he was obeying that other one," Tessa pointed out.

"He never mentioned we were here," Mia reminded her.

"We should get out of here," Noah agreed. "Let me try to see if I can call mum to let her know where we are."

He opened his phone, being careful to hide the light from the screen. "No signal."

Tessa and Mia each tried in turn, with the same result.

"Maybe it's the storm," Mia said with a tremor in her voice.

"That man got a call out," Tessa said.

"It might have been a sat phone," Noah said. "Come on, let's move. I remember where we came out. I don't want to sit out the storm. It might be dark before it ends. We'll have to go carefully. I wonder if there is any more rope around here."

Noah risked using the small torch he'd put in his pocket, and only found a twist of light rope and an old blanket. He took both.

They went out, prepared to endure the rain, knowing they had to get home before that man found them. Noah unwound the light rope and held one end by looping it around his wrist, Tessa did the same at the other end, and Mia, the slightest of them, took a twist of rope in the centre. If one of them slipped, the others could steady them. The need to step carefully kept them from thinking of the fix they were in, and Noah had his phone displaying their track up, so they could follow it back down. It was slower going down, in the very dull daylight. The occasional flash of lightning only made the track look more ominous. The cracks of thunder made them think of a predator about to pounce.

When they reached the site of the old station, they stopped to catch their breath, and to dig into their packs for the energy bars they had brought with them.

As Mia's hand touched the bag with the box they had found, she felt the familiar tug of her psychometric ability, the resonance of emotions swirling around her, thick and chaotic. She closed her eyes, allowing the feelings to wash over her. Fear, anger, desperation— they all clashed in a maelstrom that threatened to overwhelm her. As she focused, a vision flickered behind her eyelids, a flash of hands, and she knew they were Clara's, building the cairn as fear built in her, needing to finish hiding what she had done before they found her again. The sense of someone coming remained as the vision waned.

"We have to keep moving," Mia urged, her voice urgent, cutting through the tension. "I think something is watching us."

Noah had the same feeling, and instinctively took her hand, grounding her. "Then let's go. We won't let Clara's story die here."

They moved on, shadows caused by lightning loomed larger then vanished, the darkness wrapping around them like a suffocating shroud. Each rustle of leaves and snap of twigs, suggested pursuit and sent a fresh wave of anxiety coursing through Noah's veins, but he pushed it down, focusing on the path ahead.

"Do you think someone followed us from the town?" Tessa asked, her voice barely above a whisper as they pushed past wet undergrowth.

"We were looking," Noah told her. "I didn't see anyone. Did either of you sense anything."

"No," Mia told him, and Tessa echoed the answer.

"I think they have people out where we might be going. Watching, reporting. They knew where we left the bikes, but I don't think we were followed up."

"Ned implied he had," Tessa said.

"I think he was already up here," Noah gave his opinion. "He popped out of the trees opposite where we came out."

"He lied to that other man," Mia revealed. "But he did know who we were. I don't think he heard us mention Clara. But he knew he had to obey that man."

"Does that mean our bikes will be gone?" Tessa wondered.

"I don't know," Noah had to admit. "Before we try to go around the washaway, I'll try calling Mum again. She'll be worried."

The call rang, but cut out as it was answered. Noah tried again and got nothing. He tried to send a photo, the old poppet head and the picture he took of the painting of the cabin. They seemed to go.

"Come on. I will try again lower down."

They were nearly at the track around the washaway, when Noah felt his foot slip out from under him. He cried out, and Tessa had the presence of mind to move behind a tree, so the line held, and Mia didn't follow him down the slope.

"Noah! Are you okay?" Mia called, feeling some of the strain on the rope.

"Yeah, sort of," Noah called back up. "I'm trying to find somewhere it isn't so slippery."

After five minutes, the girls were getting really worried. They tried to see where Noah was, without getting too close to the edge. Both nearly screamed when they heard the voice.

"Keep back," Ned told them. "Keep pressure on that line. I've another I can toss down to help him up."

Ned knew exactly what to do, and soon a very muddy Noah was standing back on the track.

"Thanks, mate," Noah said fervently.

Ned brushed the sentiment aside. "You need to keep going. I strung a rope around the worst part, hang onto it to get around. I hid your bikes under some scrub. Told them they weren't there. Can you find your way home in this weather?"

"Yes," Noah assured him. "Have you been following us?"

"Yes."

"No one else is around? Like that nasty guy you spoke to."

"Him? I doubt it."

"What about the guy bringing a van?"

"I told him to go back to the turn off at the main road. I have to join him there. I said I was checking a couple of places you might be sheltering."

"What do they want with us?" Tessa asked.

Ned didn't answer. "If you are okay to go, do. I will follow and remove this rope."

"Can we talk to you tomorrow? Somewhere?" Noah asked.

"Better you don't," Ned told him. "Better you don't come back this way."

"Clara had a place up here, didn't she?" Mia asked. "An old miner's place. Do you know where it is?"

"You don't want to go there. There's nothing there of hers. Hurry now, but be careful."

Noah gave the others a shrug. It was back to teeming, but they were already so wet it made little difference, though Mia was beginning to shiver. When they got past the washaway, he'd give her the blanket to put around her. Meanwhile, he hoped the muck he'd collected was being washed off.

The eerie feeling followed them, but they hoped Ned was right, no other watchers were around. They were grateful for the rope, to get past the worst of the track, particularly the stretch where a river seemed to be roaring down the upslope incline.

Chapter 13: Out of Touch

Noah went to check the history trail. It seemed deserted. He went back to where they had their bikes.

"Maybe we should walk back," Tessa suggested. If any of them are around, they might hear or see the bikes."

"I tried ringing Dad," Mia told him. "My phone is dead. I think it got wet."

"Mine too," Tessa admitted.

Noah expected his to be in the same condition. When he looked at it, it was on and had two missed calls. He tried to call his mum but it didn't connect. He decided to try texting.

"Tessa, do you still have the map?"

"It will be soaked. Everything in by bag is."

"I just want to get the grid location of this place."

Tessa retrieved the soggy map with great care and opened it even more carefully. Noah used his tiny torch to find the figures he wanted. He sent, 'heading back from' then the map reference, 'on Mill Haven area map.'

For good measure, although he didn't really know why, he also forwarded his photo of Clara's cabin picture.

When they dragged their bikes out, they realised all their tyres were flat.

"Slashed." Noah swore when his torch showed the damage. "We will have to walk."

Wordlessly, they pushed their bokes back out of sight, and hoped they would still be there when they were able to get back. They had to keep walking to try to warm up. They were all shivering now.

Noah's phone beeped a message. "Find cover, stay there. Coming to get you."

He read it aloud with relief. It had come from his mum's phone. Then he began to worry about his mum driving in the dark and wet.

"Let's get nearer the trail, and get under this old blanket," Noah suggested.

Without answering, the girls began to follow him. Noah recalled a little clearing and headed for it.

Right into trouble.

A figure loomed in front of him, rising from a couch. Before he could utter a sound, something dark covered his head, and an arm grabbed him as his feet were kicked out from under him. He heard two brief squeals from the girls and he cursed himself for forgetting to watch for people. He was meant to look after them.

One of the previously silent figures let out an oath. "Try that again, girl, and I'll hit you."

Tessa, Noah thought. She wasn't giving up. Neither should he. Though right then, he couldn't do anything.

Moira Bennet kept glancing out the window at the building storm. She was worried about Noah and the girls. The original forecast had been for the change to hit in the late afternoon. Her boss noticed her distraction and reassured her. "Your lad has good sense. He'll be careful."

He was sensible, Moira reminded herself. He'd left details of where he was going. The thought worked until one of the customers summoned her. She took the order pad from her apron pocket and went over.

"Can I get you something?" she asked.

"Perhaps we can do something for you," the man suggested.

Moira thought it was a pick up line she didn't intend to respond to. Then the man said, "You really should keep a firmer reign on that boy of yours. He is meddling in things he doesn't understand."

Her maternal instinct came rushing to full strength. She sensed the menace, the veiled threat.

"He is kind and sensible," Moira said simply. Had she been a dog, her hackles would have been up.

The man shrugged. The three men all looked at her as they rose, and left money on the table for what they had ordered.

Moira watched them leave, unaware she was shaking.

"Moira!" A kinder voice distracted her.

"Oh! Tom. I didn't know you were in town."

"I am not making it known. Is something wrong?"

"I...I'm not sure."

"Were those men threatening you?"

"I...they said..." She repeated their words.

"I think we need to talk. Come, I will see if Garry will let us use the room out the back."

Garry La Touche was her boss, but he simply agreed to Tom's request and called for one of the other waitresses to cover he floor.

"What has been going on?" Tom asked, looking at Garry. "You said things were stirring."

"It seems that way. I think Moira's young one and his friends are looking into Clara."

Moira's head shot up, ready to defend her son. "He did mention her. But it was nothing. His friend, Mia, had never been to Parson's Folly. The car is still there, so naturally the subject came up. The girl is an artist, so she got interested in the Wilder Girl."

Garry spoke quietly to Tom Nicholls about a few recent events. When he mentioned the fire at the repair shop, and Clarrie's 'accident', Moira burst out, "Noah might have been there if Clarrie hadn't sold the shop and given notice to his helpers."

Tom and Garry exchanged looks full of meaning. They both recognised the implications of the events.

"So, where is Noah today?" Tom asked, keeping his tone casual.

"Oh, he and the girls were checking out the history trail, on their bikes. This storm wasn't meant to come in so early."

"They have phones," Tom asked, sounding like he expected they would.

"Yes, he went off well prepared. He sent me some photos."

She dug her phone from her apron pocket. "I'm not sure where some of them are."

Moira let Tom look through them. He identified some for her.

Outside, the first powerful gust of wind, blew over the café sign and pushed it a few metres along the footpath. It drew their attention and Garry went out to retrieve the sign. Then Moira's phone beeped twice with two messages. "They are from Noah," she said.

"Try calling him," Tom suggested.

Moira pressed the speed dial number with Noah's number, but the call didn't go through.

"Could be trouble with the tower," Garry said, hearing of her lack of connection. "It's been giving trouble a lot lately. I keep telling Mayor Hirsch he needed to look into it."

"We can try again later," Tom said. "There are some natural dead spots out that way." He asked Garry, can we get a couple of cups of coffee here?"

Moira began to rise but Tom caught her wrist. "Tell me what that lad of yours has been doing. Is he behaving himself?"

"Oh, yes. He is doing well at school, was working three nights a week for Clarrie, until this past week because Clarrie sold the shop. Clarrie put in a word for him at the local spare parts place. Gave him a reference too."

Tom Nicolls, once a detective stationed in Mill Haven, used his skill at interviewing people to elicit more information from Moira that she realised she knew. He could read between the lines and see the rising undercurrent of detrimental activity.

Almost everyone thought he had retired after Clara went missing. Officially, he had retired from the Victoria Police, but in truth, he was now working with the Australian Federal Police.

"Try ringing again," Tom suggested.

Moira tried and shook her head.

Garry suggested, "Why don't you head off, Moira. I doubt we'll be busy. Everyone will be heading home to beat the rain, and you might need to pick up your son."

"I'll drive you," Tom offered. "Are you still at the same place?"

"I am," she confirmed. "And thank you, Garry. I have to admit I am a bit worried about Noah."

"We'll talk again later, Garry," Tom said, standing up and offering Moira a help up. At the door he suggested, "Wait at the door, I will bring my car up."

He rain was now teeming down, and even with her umbrella, Moira was soaked during the short dash to the car, and more so getting from the car to her front door.

"Can I come in?" Tom asked.

"Yes, I will put the heater on so we can dry out."

When they were both sitting close to the heater, drinking hot chocolate, Moira's phone pinged again.

"More pictures," she told Tom, and again let him see them.

"The old poppet head mine," he recognised. "I thought they closed that part of the track a while back."

Moira's phone rang once and stopped. "It dropped out but it was from Noah," Tom told her.

"Then he is still okay, thank God."

A short while later, it pinged.

Tom read the message, recognised the coordinates, and checked them on the local map he had picked up on the way to town, to be sure.

"He's on his way back down from the poppet head."

"He will have a long ride back in the rain," Moira said with worry in her voice.

Tom quickly sent a reply, hoping it would get through. He told Moira what he was typing.

Moira's landline rang and she stood up to go answer it. "Yes, Bethany, Noah sent me a text." She gave the gist of it. "I have an old friend here, we're going to pick them up." She covered the phone to ask Tom, "Joel Rodriguez has offered to go along."

"Yes. Tell him to meet me here. It would be better if you stayed here, so there is a warm house to return to. You are not used to this weather. I am. And if need be, you can relay messages."

"But, he's my son..."

"You can trust me," Tom assured her, already reaching for his partly dried jacket. "Can you fill a thermos with hot water? And do you have any of those individual sachets of coffee or chocolate?"

Moira reacted at once, setting the kettle back on and then heading to get towels and spare blankets."

When Joel arrived, and the two men went off in Tom's four wheel drive, Moira sent a fervent prayer skyward.

Chapter 14: In the Dark

In spite of his struggles, Noah found himself unable to free his head of the dark hood that was clinging to his face due to the rain. His hands were tied behind him somehow, and something was forcing the fabric of the hood into his mouth. He had to stop struggling since he was running out of air. After a while, he felt himself blacking out, and gave a last desperate struggle. It was hard, since he was being carried like a roll of carpet over someone's shoulder.

The next thing he knew, he was shivering so hard his teeth chattered.

"Noah!" Tessa and Mia cried out together.

He realised they were both pressing against him, but he was shivering too hard to even blush. Relief surged through him. They were both okay, well, they were both alive.

"Wh...W...," he tried to ask, what had happened.

"We were caught near where we were going to shelter," Tessa told him. "We are somewhere out of the rain." Her voice was trembling too. "

"I think it's one of the old cabins," Mia added.

"Cl...Cl..."

"I can't tell," Mia admitted bleakly. "We couldn't see the outside and what I feel now is horrible."

"Ca...Ca... Can...free," Noah tried.

"We've been trying," Mia's voice trembled, as if she was on the verge of tears.

"They used rope, but it got wet," Tessa told him. "I'm hoping if we huddle together to conserve heat, the rope might dry a bit."

"Do you remember what happened?" Mia asked, sniffing slightly.

The ambush came back to him. "Yeah."

Then he began to be able to think and wonder if the cabin they wanted to find, was the one they were in, and if it really was Clara's secret place. The picture she did of a cabin, had to be important, although Mia had sensed only 'secrets'. His hope faded when he reminded himself there were a lot of abandoned cabins and miner's shacks. They might not be anywhere near where they were caught. The location he had sent might be all wrong.

"Ph...ph...one."

"They took our phones," Tessa grouched. Went through our bags too, but didn't take anything. Our phones still wouldn't work. I said they'd got wet. One of them tried yours, but we had no idea of your password."

"They dumped us in here," Mia explained. "Hardly said anything, just not to try to run away."

"As if we could," Tessa said sarcastically. "They can't stop me trying though."

"I think they had to put us here because something else was going on. We heard low, urgent voices. Something was worrying them. Still, they don't expect anyone to find us." That was Mia giving her idea from what she sensed.

Noah didn't like the sound of that. He was even surer they were nowhere near where they left their bikes.

Instead of trying to talk again, he tried to move his hands. Tessa felt the movement and tried to move hers closer, guessing he wanted to try untying the rope.

It was something to do, Noah decided. He was still shivering, but he had warmed enough to stop his teeth bashing each other.

"Are you okay, Mia?" he asked.

After a while, she said, "No. Not really. I'm trying something my gran taught me. It's not working."

"Tell me about it?" Noah asked while his fingers worked at the knots tying Tessa's hands together. IT felt like the rope they had taken from the feed shed.

"I am trying to concentrate on a still pond and letting unwanted thoughts flow away," Mia explained.

Noah thought on that. 'Too slow,' he decided. "How about imagining those thoughts as a big bundle of something, sitting out in the pouring rain, and being washed down into a river, right into the place where those who put us here are trying to stay dry."

Tessa gave a snort. "That's almost the exact opposite of what Mia said."

"You might like to disagree," Noah said lightly, "but you haven't noticed, this isn't exactly a normal situation."

"I like it!" Mia said. "I am not feeling like being a nice, sweet... anything."

"Neither am I," Tessa agreed fervently. "Hey, I think you are getting somewhere, Noah."

Shortly after, Tessa's hands were free. Noah got her to check a pocket in his cargo pants. He'd put a pocket knife there. Tessa found it and laughed.

"Idiots! They never thought to check there."

Freeing her feet was easy, and soon after, she had her friends free.

Noah staggered to his feet, needing to steady himself against the wooden wall, while the circulation returned to his legs and feet. Once he could walk easily, he went to the door, not surprised that it wouldn't budge. There was a narrow gap all around it, so he probed it with his knife, and finding a wide section where it could not go through as far. When he found the other edge of the obstruction, he continued to probe around and found a similar obstruction on the other edge of the door.

Noah swore, "I think they barred the door on the outside."

"You're not joking, are you?" Tessa asked.

"No and I can't' see any windows."

"Use your torch," Tessa suggested. "If I can vaguely see in here, a little bit of light is coming in somewhere."

She was right, Noah realised. Apart from a gap in the roof, where rain was trickling in, soaking down between the boards of the false floor there, the top three inches of two otherwise blocked windows allowed light in. Except with the rain, the day had become very dull.

Noah checked his watch. They had been in there at least two hours. It had been about three o'clock when they'd got back to their bikes.

While he and Tessa tried to unblock the windows, with just a pocket knife and fingers, Mia was moving around the edge of the cabin's space.

"Hey!" Mia called over to them. "Come and look here."

"What is it," Tessa asked.

"I think there is a trap door here."

"Really?" She moved ahead of Noah, but needed his torch to see anything.

"You felt something?" Noah asked Mia.

"I sensed Clara, here. She ...knelt down...there." Mia pointed.

Noah tapped the spot with his fist and found the board there was loose. He wiggled it, until one end slid under the next board. A modern looking loch was revealed. Tessa immediately reached into her pocket for the keyring she carried, and found the key Mia had found in Clara's bag. They all held their breath, giving a united sigh when the key turned.

They'd found it – Clara's cache of paintings. The only thing was, they couldn't leave to take them away. Two thick flat boxes lay under the false floor. The top one was covered in dust. Their minds recalled hearing, "People will fight to keep this quiet" and "If any of us get to close to the truth, we could end up like Clara."

"What now?" Tessa voiced the vital question.

"I can feel a cold draught coming up from under there," Mia told them. "Maybe there is space under there we can crawl into."

Noah didn't think so, but he lifted out the two boxes, lay down and ducked his head. "Hey, one of you shine my torch under the floor and towards the far wall. He felt one of the girls checking his pocket, and a slender arm edging past his head.

"Good call, Mia," Noah said, his voice muffled. "I reckon the ground slopes down a bit and the false floor is laid on some supporting beams. The dirt just here is dry and soft."

Noah began to scrape the dust to either side, making more room in the centre of the opening. He inched into the space he was making. Finally he asked, "Pull me out."

Noah helped as much as he could until his head was clear of the opening. "I reckon we could get down there, but I don't know about getting out from down there."

"I think we should," Tessa urged. "I feel like a sitting duck in here."

"We are so close. I can feel Clara urging us on," Mia added.

"Okay, let's think about this. Is there any way we can hide the way down?" He had Mia shine the torch around. "Is that an old fireplace?"

Tessa went to check. "I think so, it's full of wood."

"Let's bring over what we can to here," Noah directed. "They can think we tried to get out through the roof."

He was still thinking as the got to work. "I think we can relock the lock, and hopefully it will close properly after us. If I can arrange it, maybe I can balance some of the wood to roll over the spot."

They had just finished that when they heard voices outside. The tone was urgent.

In a low voice, Noah told the girls, "Get down below, I'll hand the cases down and our bags."

Neither liked the idea, but being in the cabin suddenly seemed suffocating. As quietly as possible, the wriggled through the hole Noah had made. Tessa stayed close to get the boxes and bags. Noah waited until she was out of his way to get feet first into the hole. He relocked the lock and slid a bit further down. He moved the wood back into place, after dragging two bits of wood closer. He tried not to hurry too much, but he heard the scrape of wood on wood, and realised people were unbarring the door. He inched down the slope feeling hangs guiding him. There was no need to tell the girls to be quiet.

Tessa spoke close to his ear. "I need your torch." He gave it to her, and sensed her moving away.

The floor above rattled as heavy boots strode around.

"Where are they?" a loud voice demanded. "Did you let the brats out?"

"I didn't even know you had them here," another voice retorted. It might have been Ned.

Someone kicked at the pile of wood, scattering it. "There is no way out through the roof."

A third voice suggested, "The cleared the wood from the fireplace."

"For hell's sake, do you think they climbed up the chimney? Check the windows. The wood could be loose."

Down below, Noah led the girls towards where the stream of water was draining away and down the hill. Maybe they could get out that way, with a bit of digging, but not if anyone was around.

In spite of their dire position, hearing the panic in the voices, at their seemingly impossible escape, was mildly amusing.

"Get back here! We have to find those kids! Jeff, see if you can find tracks."

A bit later, "Ned, you'd better hope we find them, or you are going to have to explain to the leader."

"No! It's you who will have to explain. I didn't bring them here and not check it was secure."

"Well, how did they get out" You knew this was her place. You could have come here and let them out."

"They had it figured her place was nearer the mine, well away from here. If they told anyone where they were, it wouldn't be here. We're more than five kilometres from where the bikes were."

"Well go off and find them. You managed to fool them before."

The voices stopped but it sounded like someone was kicking the wood they had taken from the fireplace. That stopped and the sounds now seemed like someone was tossing the wood back into the metal framed fireplace.

"What are you doing?" a voice demanded.

"I'm going to send those kids a message, so they know their meddling will have consequences."

"We aren't to damage this place."

"What use is it? We've been over it dozens of times. If the bitch left things here, they either rotted away or were eaten by rodents. I will make sure nothing is left."

"What if they did find something?"

"How would they find anything? They were tied up and however they got free, they probably scarpered as soon as they were."

Mia edged close to Noah, and whispered, "I'm scared."

Tessa agreed, "I think they are going to burn the place down."

Noah pulled the girls closer to where the water was coming down. "They aren't thinking straight. The outside is soaking wet, so if the fire starts inside, only the dry part will burn. The floor above where we are is soaking wet."

By their trembling, the girls still weren't sure. "A fire will attract attention," Noah tried to reassure them, and himself. "Help will come, they won't stick around. We will get out of this. Mia, did you get anything off the boxes?"

"They are important. Clara was going to return for them."

"Then we need to be positive. We are going to see this through, for Clara. Right?"

"Right," Tessa agreed softly. "Should we try to start widening the hole the water made?"

"Do you think the time is right?" Mia asked.

Tessa took a breath, calming herself. "No...not yet. They have people all around this place, I can't tell how many."

"They are going to watch the place burn," Mia gasped, horrified. "But we can't end here."

Chapter 15: Rescue

Tom Nicholls drove to where the coordinates led, and not seeing Noah and his friends, headed up the closed track. He found the bikes, saw the slashed tyres and his expression hardened. He cave a call, hoping the kids had done as he asked. Joel went up further, flashing his torch to either side of the track and calling his daughter's name.

"Tom! Up here."

Joel pointed to the old blanked, and the remains of some old rope. "Now what?" He was trying to project calm. While hiding his fear for his daughter.

Tom brought up the forwarded message with the picture of a cabin. "Know where this is?"

"No idea. I'm a stockbroker. I don't go hiking. What does the picture mean?"

"One idea I had, was the young people were looking for it," Tom thought aloud. "I know there are a lot of old miner's shacks around Mill Haven. Nearly all are still abandoned. Bill Wilder brought one for a retreat. It wasn't in this area, which is right on the history trail."

"Do you think they were taken from here?"

"From here, yes."

"Why?"

"They were interested in Clara Wilder."

Joel muttered an oath. "The little idiots. So that's what this is about."

"Oh?" Tom prompted.

Joel related the anonymous allegations about his daughter and how she had responded. "I have no reason to doubt her, and the other two were almost run down by a guy on a push bike."

"And Clarrie was warned to leave town. He didn't go fast enough," Tom murmured.

"They should have left things alone," Joel growled.

"What have they threatened you with?" Tom asked.

"How..."

"It's how the people behind this operate," Tom explained. "You don't have to tell me. Your reaction was all I needed. I would say that nearly everyone in town has been threatened in some way, by someone who has eyes everywhere in town. I know. They even tried it with me."

"And you left town."

"Yes. They would have kept watching me and made it impossible for me to investigate them. I promised Bill Wilder I'd look after Clara if something happened to him. I failed them both, but I intend to find the person, or people, that are putting undeserved fear into everyone in town."

"Do they know you are back?"

Tom chuckled. "No, but this talk isn't helping. My question is do we waste time around here looking for a cabin, or aim for the one in the photo?"

"You probably know best," Joel decided.

"Then I need to call in some reinforcements."

"Can you trust them?"

"With my life," Tom said soberly. "I still have friends here who keep me advised of goings on. Several incidents alerted me. If my target is moving against people now, after ten years of quiet, he is still very worried."

Tom made one call, gave a brief explanation, and mentioned a place to meet. "Come on. We are meeting at the mini-rail station."

Joel kept with Tom Nicholls once he had given instructions to the twelve people who had arrived within half an hour. It seemed they had been warned to move out at a moment's notice. From the voices, he knew they weren't all men. Who they were, he had no idea. They all wore waterproof dark outfits, and had an air of quiet competence. When Tom had finished outlining his plan, they all moved off to forma a cordon around the hut that had once belonged to Bill Wilder. The rain did not seem to deter them.

"Shouldn't we be calling the police?" Joel asked as they moved through wet forest.

"I am the police," Tom murmured.

Tom used the GPS on his phone to guide him, and a torch with the light covered in red, to provide a little more light. When he stopped, Joel almost walked into him, but then heard voices arguing. A loud 'crack', not from thunder, ended the dispute.

"I smell smoke," Joel murmured.

Tom sent a text. "Move in."

To Joel, he said, "Keep back a bit. If we encounter people, be prepared to stop them getting past."

"Right!" he said quietly. He was determined to help. Seeing flickering red light inside the structure, served to fuel his anger. He wanted to rush in to be sure his daughter was not inside, but then he could be hurt and the people up ahead might get away.

He was startled when a short burst of a siren came from beyond the shack. Without anyone shouting orders, the men watching the shack, turned to run.

Tom took one down before the man knew he was there. The second tried to dodge and never saw what tripped him, certainly felt the weight pinning him down until his hands were tied.

"Watch them," Tom instructed, as he listened through some kind of headpiece. He counted the reports of captures and hoped they had them all. He was already moving in on the cabin, hoping he wasn't too late.

Flames were drying out the walls and roof, and the outside was beginning to smoulder. He threw open the door, shone his uncovered light around, and saw no sign of captives or bodies. He called out anyway, but got no reply.

He spun around when he heard, "They weren't in there. They got out somehow."

Tom shone his torch on the speaker's blood covered face. "You're one of them."

"I didn't want to be, if I didn't obey, they said they would reveal proof I'd..."

"Ted Thornton," Tom guessed.

"They call me Ned. They change all our names."

"Why didn't you run off?"

"I'm too dizzy, and I'd had enough."

A sharp 'crack' and a shower of bright orange sparkles, had Tom running to the back of the structure, fearing the worst. Then he began grinning in relief as he saw three teenagers standing defiantly in the grip of two of his team. In the torch light, it wasn't hard to read their body language. He gestured to one of the men. "Go find my partner. You wait with the two prisoners, but tell him to come here."

Tessa saw her father and jerked free to run to him. Noah put an arm around Mia, then turned to the new arrival. "Who are you?"

"Tom Nicholls." He reached for his ID.

"We know who you are. What did you write at the vigil for Clara?" Noah asked.

The words came immediately. Heartfelt and not forgotten.

Mia told him, "We have Clara's paintings. We don't know what they will prove, but it's how she recorded what she found out."

"What you three young people did, was dangerous, but I commend your courage."

Mia said, having already decided Tom could be trusted, "My grandma, Lilac Chang, told me I would know when someone needed help."

Tom recognised the name and a piece of a puzzle fell into place. "I am going to get you three home, warmed up and dry. Then if you are up to it, we need to talk."

"Yes," Noah agreed, a sentiment echoed by Mia and Tessa. "We will be Clara's voice."

News of a police raid somewhere near Mill Haven, leaked out causing locals to congregate in little huddles and look around fearfully. Details were not available. The local reporters tried to find out what and where. The local police contingent were under orders to say nothing, discuss it with no one.

Fortunately, word of the part Noah, Mia and Tessa had played, and their ordeal, had not leaked out. With the permission of their parents, Tom had taken them to a place, one town over, provided them with new prepaid phones, as their own had been found on one of the men arrested and were currently evidence.

Their parents were to act worried if anyone asked them

questions, and each allowed their phones to be monitored.

The three teenagers missed a week of school while Tom went over everything they had done, found, considered or thought of. Except for their families, everyone that knew them thought their absence was suspicious and rumours spread around town.

Yet behind the rumours, a lot was happening. The new leads provided by the very observant teenagers were proving valid and important.

Tom opened up Clara's sketches for the first time in ten years. Then, knowing of Lilac Chang, did not question the unexpected observations Mia made when she touched each one. Clara's journals, her picture descriptions, and the pictures themselves, correlated time after time with police reports that were made and forgotten.

Mia mentioned the roll of small pages, the odd key and the metal tube. These went to the police lab and were vital pieces of evidence. Tom didn't explain in detail, just that the key looked to be for a safe, and the tube contained a pernicious type of drug.

In a dozen instances, the police went to the site of one of Clara's pictures and found new evidence of a crime, long buried. The area of the cairn, where Mia had found the lunchbox, was searched and a skeleton was recovered. The picture, gave then a clue to the identity, which was later proved by dental records and DNA. The mystery disappearance of a young heiress, over ten years before, was now solved.

Warrants were issued, raids authorised, and arrests were made. The inhabitants of Mill Haven woke to read a special edition of the local paper – and the tentative hope that a twenty year reign of terror was finally over.

Chapter 16: The Truth Revealed

The heavy oak doors of Mill Haven's town hall creaked open, allowing a trickle of anxious townsfolk to drift inside, their murmurs mingling with the low hum of fluorescent lights overhead. Noah stood at the front of the room, his heart thumping like a rapid drumbeat in his chest. He exchanged nervous glances with Mia and Tessa, feeling the weight of their collective resolve as they prepared to confront the ghosts of their past. The air was thick with apprehension, punctuated by the lingering scent of old paper and varnished wood.

"Are you ready?" Tessa whispered, her voice barely breaking the tension that enveloped them.

Noah nodded, though he wasn't sure if it was more to reassure her or himself. He took a deep breath, inhaling the familiar scent of dust and history, and stepped forward, his hands trembling slightly as he adjusted the stack of papers he held. Behind him, Mia fidgeted with Clara's journal, her fingers brushing over the worn leather cover, as if drawing strength from the connection to the woman she thought of as a lost friend.

Tom Nicholls stood on the stage, at the microphone. People recognised him, and nudged their neighbours. Silence fell, as everyone hoped to hear more of the dramatic events of the previous weeks.

"This evening would never had come about, if not for the courage and determination of three of our next generation of adults, and their belief in one this town has shunned unjustly during her life here, and since. It is thanks to them that the shadow that has hovered over this town has been lifted. Please welcome Noah, Tessa and Mia."

All eyes went to the youngsters on the stage. Faces betrayed a range of emotions, but they were all prepared to listen. Tom stepped back and Noah reached the microphone.

"Tonight, we seek to honour the memory of Clara Wilder who uncovered the truth that has haunted Mill Haven for far too long,"

Noah's voice rang out, steadying as he began to address the gathering crowd. The dim lighting cast shadows across the faces that turned toward him, a mix of curiosity and scepticism flickering in their eyes.

He glanced across the room, spotting familiar faces among the crowd—Mr. Jensen, the elderly baker, his white hair a halo of softness, and Mrs. Thompson, Clara's old art teacher, her eyes glistening with unshed tears. Yet, there were also those who wore expressions of hardened disbelief, like old stones worn smooth by relentless tides. Noah felt their scrutiny, the weight of years of secrets pressing down upon him.

Looking at his notes, he began to tell those present of what he, along with his friends, found and some of what it led to. He mentioned Clara's journal, and her paintings, then stepped to one side.

Mia stepped beside him, her petite frame almost swallowed by the bulk of the podium, and cleared her throat. "Clara came to be like a friend," she said, her voice trembling yet resolute. "She deserves to be remembered for who she truly was, not just as a name whispered in the dark. A person blamed for all the ills in the town."

A ripple of murmurs cascaded through the crowd, and a pair of sceptical elders exchanged glances, their faces etched with lines of worry and disdain. "Perhaps some things are better left buried," one of them muttered, his voice low but heavy with authority.

Tessa leaned in closer, her bright green eyes flashing with determination. "We can't let fear silence us anymore. Clara's story isn't just hers; it's ours too. It's part of this community."

The room felt charged, the air thickening with the unspoken emotions that clung to the walls like old paint. Noah glanced at Mia, whose dark eyes sparkled with unshed tears, and he could see her resolve hardening, transforming her vulnerability into a fierce determination. She held Clara's journal aloft, the pages fluttering slightly in her grasp, and turned to the projector screen behind them.

"Clara wrote this," she said, her voice gaining strength. "It's filled with her thoughts, her dreams, and the moments that made her who she was." As she began to read, the room fell silent, the townsfolk drawn in by the intimacy of Clara's words, the raw honesty that spilled from the pages like an open wound.

"'I wish I could tell everyone how much I love this town...'" Mia's voice wavered slightly, but she pressed on, the words wrapping around the crowd like a warm embrace. "...'and how much I want to be seen for who I really am.'"

For a moment, a palpable sense of connection formed, as if Clara's spirit had threaded through the very air they breathed. But just as hope began to blossom, it was torn asunder by a sharp voice cutting through the silence.

"How dare you bring this up again?" A figure emerged from the back, his silhouette dark against the light. Lucas, Clara's former friend, stormed forward, his face twisted with anger. "You think dredging up the past will change anything? Clara was no saint!"

Noah's stomach dropped. He had known Lucas would come; he had felt it in the pit of his gut. "We're not here to judge her," Noah said, stepping forward, his voice steady. "We're here to let the truth set her free!"

The crowd began to murmur again, the buzz of conversation escalating into a chaotic din. People shifted uncomfortably, caught between their memories of Clara and the fierce accusations being hurled. Noah could see the uncertainty in their eyes, the struggle within their hearts. They wanted to remember Clara, but they were also terrified of what that meant.

Lucas pointed an accusatory finger, his voice rising above the clamour. "You think you can rewrite history? Clara may have been your friend, but she was complicated. She hurt people!"

Mia flinched, the words striking her like a physical blow. Tessa stepped forward, her athletic frame poised and ready to defend. "Everyone has a story, Lucas. Clara's story didn't end ten years ago. We're giving her the voice she never had!"

The room fell silent again, the tension coiling tighter than a spring. Noah glanced at Mia, her eyes wide with determination, and he felt a surge of solidarity. "We're not just here for Clara," he added, addressing the townsfolk. "We're here for all of us. We've all been touched by those who silenced her, and we owe it to her to see the truth."

Gradually, some of the townsfolk began to nod, their expressions softening as memories surfaced. An older woman in the back stood up, her voice trembling. "Clara was my student. She had such promise, such talent. I never wanted to forget her."

"Yes!" another voice chimed in from the crowd. "She deserves justice, not silence!"

Encouraged by the rising tide of support, Noah stepped back to Mia and Tessa, their bond solidifying in the shared mission. As the crowd began to stir with renewed energy, he felt a surge of hope. This wasn't just about Clara; it was about the community reclaiming its narrative, facing its past, and healing together.

But Lucas wasn't finished. He charged forward, eyes blazing with defiance. "You think you can just rewrite what happened? The truth is ugly, and it won't change just because you want it to!"

Noah took a deep breath, his heart racing. "Then let us face the ugly truth together. All the ugly truths," he replied, his voice firm. "None of us is a saint, but how Clara was treated is more than any single person should have to bear. How many people helped her when she needed help? Your brother was one, and he didn't deserve to die. We owe it to Clara, and we owe it to ourselves, to forgive each other."

The tension in the room hung heavy, but slowly, the townsfolk began to voice their own memories, sharing snippets of laughter, regret, and sorrow. Each story wove a tapestry of shared experience, binding them together in a way they had long forgotten. The air was electric with emotions, rising and falling like the tide.

As Lucas fell silent, the realization of his isolation etched into his features, Noah stepped back, allowing the townsfolk to take the stage. An older man spoke up, his voice gravelly but resolute. "I remember Clara painting by the old fountain, her laughter echoing through the square. We can't forget that. She deserves to be remembered for the joy she brought us, not just to be blamed for the troubles she did not give us, or be gratified by her disappearance."

Mia beamed at Noah, pride swelling within her. Tessa caught his eye and nodded, her expression fierce. This was it—the moment they had worked so hard for. Clara's memory was being reclaimed, not just as a ghost of the past but as a vibrant part of their community.

The meeting continued with voices rising and blending, passion igniting as they shared memories, laughter, and pain. It was chaotic, raw, and beautiful. Noah felt the walls of silence begin to crumble, and in their place, a new understanding took root—a recognition of their shared humanity and the importance of letting go of fear.

Finally, the meeting began to wind down, the Mayor took the microphone and announced a day of celebration with special events which would be held the following week, and to watch the paper for details.

The townsfolk began slowly dispersing, some with tears still glistening in their eyes, others with newfound determination. As the last few stragglers exited, Noah, Mia, and Tessa stepped outside into the cool night air. The stars twinkled above, illuminating the path ahead, and a sense of relief washed over Noah.

"We did it," Mia breathed, looking up at the sky, her voice a whisper of awe.

Tessa squeezed Noah's hand, her smile bright against the darkness. "We're not finished yet. There's still more to do."

Noah nodded, feeling a flicker of hope blossom within him. "Yeah, but we took the first step."

As they walked away from the town hall, hand in hand, Tessa paused, a distant look in her eyes. "I just had a vision," she said softly, her voice trembling. "Clara... she's smiling. I think she's finally at peace."

The three of them stood together, the cool breeze wrapping around them like a protective cloak, and in that moment, Noah felt an unshakeable bond form between them—stronger than the secrets that had once divided their town. They were a part of something greater now, a community united in the quest for truth and healing.

"Sometimes," he mused, glancing at his friends, "unveiling the past is the first step toward healing the future."

And as they stepped into the night, the weight of Clara's memory settled gently on their shoulders, no longer a burden but a guiding light leading them toward reconciliation.

Chapter 17: Healing and New Beginnings

The sun hung low in the sky, casting a golden sheen across the once shunned field, where the wildflowers danced playfully in the gentle late summer breeze. Noah leaned against the hood of the rusty old car, its faded paint glinting like a relic of the past. The car had become more than just a vessel of memories; it was a testament to their journey—a journey that had unearthed secrets and mended some of the town's deepest wounds. He could still hear the echoes of the town meeting from the night before, a blend of whispers, gasps, and the occasional supportive cheer.

"Can you believe how many people showed up?" Mia's voice broke through his reverie, her dark hair pulled back in a loose ponytail, strands framing her face as she perched herself beside him. The wind tousled her hair, and she tucked it behind her ear, her almond-shaped eyes sparkling with a mixture of hope and uncertainty.

"No," Noah replied, shaking his head. "I thought half the town would still be too scared to talk." He glanced toward the town where the meeting had taken place, and even so far from it, the air still seemed to be buzzing with remnants of the conversations that had unfolded there. "But I guess Clara's story really struck a chord."

Tessa approached, her long legs carrying her swiftly over the uneven grass, her curly chestnut hair bouncing with each step. "You should have seen the looks on their faces when we revealed the truth."

She hopped up onto the car's hood, sitting cross-legged, her bright green eyes alight with enthusiasm.

"That it was the former Mayor, who was behind all their tormenting fears. That he was the master of an enclave of lost souls, so close to here but no one ever spoke of. I thought old Mr. Peterson was going to faint!"

Mia laughed, a melodic sound that danced in the warm air. "Right? He didn't even know what to say. I mean, it's not every day you find out that the town's biggest so called philanthropist, a man he staunchly supported, was the cause of so many despicable events. The mysterious culprit was hidden right under our noses."

While Noah admitted a degree of sympathy for the old man, he felt a stronger swell of pride as he listened to his friends. They had faced the unknown together, digging deep into the heart of Mill Haven's past, confronting not just the mystery of Clara but the shadows that had loomed over the town for years. "But it's not just about Clara anymore," he said, glancing at his friends. "It's about everyone who was affected by what happened. They need to heal, just like we do."

Tessa nodded thoughtfully. "Change doesn't happen overnight. But last night felt like the first step. People are finally talking, sharing their memories. I overheard Mrs. Albright telling stories about how Clara used to paint the town with her laughter, how she brought everyone together."

Mia's smile faded slightly as she looked down at her hands. "But what if it doesn't last? There are still people who think we shouldn't have brought it up at all."

Noah placed a reassuring hand on her shoulder. "We can't control how they react, but we can keep the conversation going. We've opened the door; now we just have to keep pushing it until it swings wide."

A silence settled among them, each lost in their thoughts. The remembered sounds of laughter and conversation from the park drifted into their little bubble, filling the space with a sense of community that had been absent for too long.

"Speaking of keeping the conversation going," Tessa said, her voice breaking the stillness as she hopped off the car, "what are we going to do with this momentum? We can't just let it fizzle out. We need to do something to honour Clara's memory, to show the town we care."

Mia's eyes lit up as an idea began to take shape. "What if we started a community project? Like a mural or a garden. Something that symbolizes new beginnings and healing."

Noah's heart raced at the thought. "A mural could be amazing! We could involve everyone—kids, adults, even the sceptical ones. It would give them a chance to share their stories, their memories of Clara."

"I love it," Tessa exclaimed, her excitement infectious. "We could hold workshops, get people involved in the design process. It could be a way to bring the community together."

Mia looked between her friends, her heart swelling with gratitude for their unwavering support. "I want to paint it," she declared, her voice steady. "I want to capture Clara's spirit and the essence of Mill Haven. It needs to be vibrant, alive."

"Then let's make it happen," Noah said, a newfound determination sparking within him. "We'll present the idea at the special town meeting to plan the celebration. We can show them that we're serious about healing and honouring Clara's legacy."

As they discussed their plans, the sun dipped lower in the sky, painting the horizon in strokes of orange and pink. The world around them felt alive, pulsating with possibility. They were no longer just kids tangled in a mystery; they were catalysts for change, ready to reshape their community.

The returned to the road, to where they had left their bikes, and saw a car parked there, and Tom Nicholls resting against it. Without a word, they drew closer to him.

"You did a good thing last night," he commended. "And thanks to you, more than a dozen families will be reunited with loved ones they mourned as dead."

"I don't understand," Mia admitted.

"Those slips of paper you found, had messages. They used an old fashioned means to hide it. They used lemon juice so they looked blank, but over time the paper turned brown. We had names of the forgotten ones. Some, are now dead, but not all. I have one with me that wanted to thank you in person."

The figure that stepped from the car was at first a stranger, but a moment later, both Mia and Tessa asked, "Clara?"

The woman smiled at all of them. She moved first to Mia, and gave her a hug of pure gratitude. "I am sorry to hear that your gran is gone, but it was because of her that I had the courage to endure. I held onto her promise that one day the truth would be revealed."

Then Clara drew both Tessa and Noah into a hug. "Thank you, all of you, for making it happen."

"Will you be coming back to town?" Mia asked. "You already

feel like a friend and I don't want to lose that."

Clara looked at each of them and asked, "Would you understand if I said I won't be making it known I am still alive?"

No one had an answer.

"It's just that I think the town will heal faster if I am not right there as a reminder of the past. It is enough for me that I am no longer remembered with enmity I never deserved. I long since forgave everybody, for I know, probably better than anyone, who was to blame. Once I have done my part in sending that one and the worst of his followers to well-deserved justice, I will be going away to start a new life with a new name."

"Will you find a way to keep in touch?" Mia pleaded.

Clara smiled. "I will, when I have settled."

"What about all your pictures?" Tessa asked.

"Once they are no longer needed as evidence, they will be my gift to you."

"We were talking of doing a mural, or a garden, something to symbolise a new beginning and healing," Noah told her. "I think it would be fitting if a small part of that mural was something you have painted."

A real smile blossomed on Clara's face. "I would really love that, though I have not painted for a very long time. It will be a way for me to help the healing too. It will give me something special to do while the trials drag on. When will you need it?"

"We haven't broached the idea with the council yet, we only just thought if the idea. We will have to design something…"

Mia suddenly smiled and said, "I have the very idea."

"I wish you didn't need to go," Tessa blurted, sensing that she needed to be away.

"So do I, but you are my friends and I won't forget that."

As Tom Nicholls drove away, Mia shared her idea, and they discussed possible variations. The idea had taken root and their excitement grew. Then a shadow crept over Mia's face.

"Noah," she said quietly, her voice barely above a whisper, "can we talk about something else? Something that's been on my mind?"

Noah turned to her, the weight of her words settling between them like a fragile glass. "Of course. What's on your mind?"

Mia hesitated, her gaze drifting toward the horizon, as if searching for the right words among the clouds. "It's about us," she finally said, her voice steadying. "I've been thinking a lot about what happened during our adventure and how it's changed everything between us."

Noah's pulse quickened, the air around them thick with unspoken tension. "What do you mean?"

"I mean... I've had feelings for you for a long time, Noah," she confessed, biting her lip. "But I didn't want to ruin our friendship. And now, with everything that's happened, I just don't know where we stand."

Tessa watched them with an intensity that felt both supportive and slightly uncomfortable, the air thick with anticipation. Noah's heart raced, a mix of fear and exhilaration coursing through him. "Mia, I—"

Before he could finish, Tessa jumped in. "Wait! We should be talking about this together. The three of us. We're a team, right?"

Mia nodded but didn't take her eyes off Noah. "I just need to know how you feel, Noah. I can't pretend anymore."

Noah swallowed hard, his mind racing. He felt the weight of Tessa's gaze alongside Mia's intense expectation. "I care about you both so much," he started, words tumbling out in a rush. "And yeah, I've been feeling something between us too, Mia. But I didn't want to complicate things. I didn't want to lose what we have."

Mia's breath caught, and Tessa's expression softened, her protective demeanour shifting to one of understanding. "We wouldn't lose each other," Tessa said gently. "We can work through this together."

"Exactly," Noah added, his heart pounding in his chest. "We can figure this out. I don't want to make things weird, but I also don't want to ignore what's happening between us."

Mia's face broke into a tentative smile, relief washing over her like a soothing balm. "So, we're okay? We can talk about this more?"

"Definitely," Noah said, his voice firm. "Just—give me some time to process everything, okay?"

"Of course," Mia replied, her eyes sparkling again. "I just didn't want to keep hiding how I feel."

Tessa clapped her hands together, breaking the moment's tension.

"Okay, so we have a mural to plan and feelings to sort through. Let's not lose sight of all the good that's happening."

As the sun began its final descent, the trio stood together, the world around them radiant with promise. They were bound not only by the secrets they had uncovered but by the evolving nature of their friendship, a journey that now included the tangled threads of love and vulnerability. With a newfound sense of purpose.

They each mounted their bikes and made their way back to the town, laughter and warmth spilling into the air as they rode, they felt ready to embrace whatever came next.

Epilogue

As they joined the gathering in the park, they could see townsfolk sharing stories, laughter echoing through the warm afternoon air. Their dream of a memorial to symbolise hope for the future, was already taking shape. A garden surrounded by murals painted by those moved by the story of Clara. Not all the murals were finished, but as they were they were mounted under a protective roof, with a plaque sharing the inspiration for the picture, and the artist. They were currently covered, waiting for the official unveiling when all were finished. Mia had almost finished her contribution, a dream like painting of Clara as she had been and as she was now. It would form a back drop to a sculptured diorama of historical landmarks, that had also been places Clara had been, In one section, would be the painting that had arrived from Clara, a flock of birds rising from a rough miners cottage.

A member of the council was explaining the plans to remember Clara's gifts to the town, nearby, people were finally opening up and recognising her sacrifice.

If around then it looked more like a festival, no one found it wrong. It was a time for joy.

Noah exchanged glances with Mia and Tessa, their smiles reflecting the hope that had begun to bloom in Mill Haven. They had opened a door, and as they stepped through it together, they felt the weight of the past begin to lift, revealing a brighter future waiting just beyond the horizon.

"Let's show them what we can do," Noah said, his voice filled with determination as they joined the gathering, ready to be part of the change they had started.

The End

ERIN: THE FORCING OF WISDOM
For years, Erin has used the intricacies of cyberspace to banish unwanted emotions. Others call what she does hacking, and her manipulations criminal, but now her skill was exceptional - in, out, traceless. She was wrong. Someone betrayed her.
Travis has dangerous plans. He needs an electronics expert – one he can coerce through fear. Erin was perfect.
With the inescapable threat of prison looming, Erin accepts his offer of sanctuary. When she realises his intentions, she is in too deep. But the terrifying of innocents is unforgivable. She cannot walk away. She is an empath and shares their distress. She has to help them, even if it means prison, and insanity...

ERIN: THE CALL
(including ELISABETH AND TANYA: BLOOD CALLS TO BLOOD.
Elisabeth's sister, Wanda, had been missing for half a year. Multiple authorities had found no trace of her, or her two colleagues. Yet she knew her sister was still alive and had answered a call for help from an alien who had once lived on Earth.
Elisabeth, along with her newly found cousin Tanya, have started to sense things from her missing sister. Enough to know that she is in dire trouble, but not enough to help her.
While looking for traces of the aliens, Elisabeth makes some unexpected discoveries about her family. Yet even with the help of a second newly discovered cousin, she fears she is not strong enough to help her sister and the others to return.

ERIN: THE CALL
Convicted cyber-criminal, Erin Mason, is startled into awareness in an unfamiliar place, with no memory of escaping and only vague memories of getting there. Voices in her head were urging her to go west, and they were getting more urgent.
After a chance meeting with covert agent, Jim Phillips, when she helped save his mission, he realised that she might be the key to another, more personal quest – to find three missing state department agents.
All he must do is keep Erin safe, and hide her from an intense police search, until he can introduce her to cousins she was unaware of.
However her uncontrolled psychic gifts conflict with a logical mind that prefers the ordered intricacies of computers and electronics. She only wants to shut out the voices and the madness she sees looming.
Can Phillips convince her to help him, before the forces of the law find her?

THE SERPENT'S SHADOW
Three books in one.
Janna consorts with terrorists to protect her friend Prince Ali from assassins.
Former cyber-criminal, Erin, becomes part of the merchandise of stolen tech secrets.
Jim Phillip's team is sent to neutralise the leader of the terrorist Cobra Sect.

ROYAL FAVOUR
A quick in-out investigation by US State Department agent, Wanda Martin, is compromised when she is caught after an illicit survey of an ultra-private club. When she should have been gone, team leader Jim Phillips, must organise medical help for her serious wounds as well as adapting his plans to thwart a traitor wishing to turn a tiny European Kingdom into a haven for international crooks

FOREIGN AGENT - THIEF
When US Trade Consul, Allan Wexford, and his daughter go missing, Wanda Martin flies to Austria to find them. Operating on her own, using old and new skills, she begins to unobtrusively unravel Wexford's movements. In spite of all her skill, she becomes a person of interest to both the police and a group of violent criminals, and she is set up to take the fall for a heinous crime.

PRISONER - SPY
On remand for murders she didn't commit and a robbery she never intended to do, Wanda Martin tries to keep from thinking of the inevitable outcome. Yet it is soon apparent that the Russian crime family, whose plans she wrecked, want revenge, and even in prison she isn't safe.

KORVU: THE BEGINNING
Jai Ansuni was the first female Atapi sorcerer for thousands of years, but she dare not reveal it. However, when tribal sorcerer, Stacion Ansuni escalates the enmity between Atapi and Kumatan to an ominous level. Jai and her womb mate, Con, try to mitigate his atrocities but can two young Atapi, not even a score of years old, win against the powerful sorcerer?

THE WILD ONE
Sixteen year old Jai Cassidy thought she was finally free of her family until she is discovered by her other relatives...the ones that aren't human. Jai uses her natural perversity and cunning to escape their control, but catapults herself into the middle of a deadly feud between two alien races.

ATAPI SORCERESS
Jai Cassidy is beginning her mission of reversing the decline of the non-humanoid Atapi. As a sorceress and an Atapi-Human hybrid, she is vehemently disliked by the male Atapi sorcerers and the humanoid rulers of Korvu. Her task is complicated by the treachery of a group of alien engineers, who are inciting insurrection and harsh reprisals.

THE TYMOREAN TRUST BOOK 1 - POWER RISING
The Tymorean Trust - When peace rules Tymorea - Peace reigns in the universe.
Chosen to be the Advocates of the mystical and incorporeal Guardians of Peace, twins Tymos and Kryslie must first learn to control and use the power rising in them - or it will destroy them.
On Tymorea, only the ruling Triumvirate Governors are powerful enough to guide the strong-willed alien-bred twins until they have mastered their power.

THE TYMOREAN TRUST BOOK 2 - GREAT ONES
The peace of the Guardian Planet, Tymorea, is in deadly peril. War there will create ripples of unrest and destruction throughout the settled universe. Tymos and Kryslie, still adolescents, have barely mastered their power and Llaimos is still less than a year old, but they are the three chosen to be Advocates of the mystical Guardians of Peace, to safeguard the Tymorean Trust.

THE TYMOREAN TRUST BOOK 3 - RETURN TO EARTH
Even before the war on Tymorea, the Elders foresaw that Great Ones Tymos and Kryslie would have an imperative mission on Earth.
But as the Tymoreans prepare to build an Earthbase to support them, they discover that specifications for two vital protective shields are missing.
Now, nearly a century later, Tymos and Kryslie must find his work and build the generator before the base is found.

THE TYMOREAN TRUST BOOK 4 - EARTH MISSION
Just before their graduation from the prestigious WSRA Washington University, Tymos and Kryslie Ward deliberately disappear.
The Great Ones have foreseen the capture and death of the new Tymorean missionaries and discovered that the leader of the Eastern Imperium plans to undermine the United World Nations.
Tymos and Kryslie must protect their kin and prevent a potentially devastating world war.

THE TYMOREAN TRUST BOOK 5 – ALIEN CONTACT
Tymos and Kryslie Ward, hide their Tymorean intelligence and abilities
while working as low ranked technicians at the WSRA's lunar base. When
an alien ship arrives at Lunar One, pursued by a powerful enemy who will
stop at nothing to get what he wants, only the two Tymorean Great Ones
have the knowledge and abilities to overcome him, but to do so they must
risk their sanity, and their souls.

THE TYMOREAN TRUST BOOK 6 – INVASION
Great Ones Tymos and Kryslie go to rescue the crew of Earth's first deep
space mission – and discover that Ciriot space pirates have discovered
Earth's location. When the Ciriot invade in force, the Great Ones reveal
themselves so that Earth can gain vital help. However, Kryslie becomes
the victim of Ciriot, who want to control her mind and make her betray
the people of Earth.

TRICKS
Tom and Jo Dwyer had a reputation for playing tricks – and getting
detention. They didn't seem to care about that, so long as they made their
class laugh. That was until someone began to turn their tricks against
them, and it was no longer funny.

THE CHANCE TO BE ME
Orphan Brenda Jacobs finds herself travelling to a strange town to spend
the summer holidays, but trouble finds her there and the actions of her
relatives make her life seem bleak. Then an unexpected discovery totally
changes her future.

THE MAGPIE'S DAUGHTER
Andy is almost 18 and free of her brother. Outwardly honest, Martin was
really a crook, but she didn't dare prove it. When she runs away, Martin
comes after her. Owing money, he wants her inheritance. What can Andy
do when his enemies find her?

HOLDER OF SECRETS 1 - UNREGARDED
Just out of a girl's training centre, 17 YO Peg Jessup returns home to rural
Victoria. Loath to be sent back, and unwilling to be bullied, Peg decides to
straighten out her aunt. In the process, she learns of her aunt's relationship
to dangerous men, and oddities about her own origins. When the men
realise her aunt had kept secrets from them, Peg also becomes a target.
The story is set in the 70s.

HOLDER OF SECRETS 2 - UNSUSPECTED
After barely escaping death, Peg Jessup and friend Jack, go north for a new start. Peg's nascent musical talent impels them to Tamworth and leads to a fantastic opportunity. Now called Megan, she learns of shares bequeathed by her mother and the deadly interest of two rival companies. When unwanted attention falls on her, her fledgling career is put in jeopardy. The story is set in the 1970s.

HOLDER OF SECRETS 3 - UNREPENTANT
Targeted by criminals who fear the end of their unopposed reign of terror, the former Peg Jessup, now Megan Dawes, intends to fight back. Odd things revealed by her aunt and items she saved from her aunt's house, give the police new leads to facts that could put the men away for life. The same information provides further surprises about her own origins. The story is set in the early 1970s.

MAEVEN DRAGON THIEF
Running away from an arranged marriage, Princess Maeven decides to become a thief. But was it choice or destiny? For when the kingdom faces grave peril, her skills are needed, and the dying dragon mage has chosen her to protect her successor.

MAEVEN DRAGON AGENT
When Maeven threw herself between her son and the ruthless demon, Ciabolo, her twisty tongue didn't save her. Captured and taken to the citadel of the kingdom's enemies, she uses her skills of thief and spy to learn their secrets.

MAEVEN DRAGON CHAMPION
Maeven wakes to find her body possessed by a powerful demon. Only when he sleeps, can she act - to be a thief and spy within the enemy's citadel. Can her kin oust the demon from her body so she can reveal his weaknesses?